OF TRITON

OF TRITON

ANNA BANKS

FEIWEL AND FRIENDS
NEW YORK

A FEIWEL AND FRIENDS BOOK
An Imprint of Macmillan

FEIWEL AND FRIENDS BOOKS MAY BE PURCHASED FOR BUSINESS OR PROMOTIONAL USE.
FOR INFORMATION ON BULK PURCHASES, PLEASE CONTACT THE MACMILLAN
CORPORATE AND PREMIUM SALES DEPARTMENT AT (800) 221-7945 × 5442 OR
BY E-MAIL AT SPECIALMARKETS@MACMILLAN.COM.

LIBRARY OF CONGRESS CATALOGING-IN-PUBLICATION DATA AVAILABLE

ISBN: 978-1-250-00333-1 (HARDCOVER) / 978-1-250-04245-3 (EBOOK)

FEIWEL AND FRIENDS LOGO DESIGNED BY FILOMENA TUOSTO

FIRST EDITION: 2013

10 9 8 7 6 5 4 3 2 1

MACTEENBOOKS.COM

For Tami

OF TRITON

1

MY EYES won't open. It's like my lashes are coated with iron instead of mascara, pulling down my lids with a heaviness I can't fight. A medicated kind of heaviness.

I'm disoriented. Part of me feels awake, as if I'm swimming from the bottom of the ocean to the surface, but my body feels floaty, like I'm already there rolling with the lull of the waves.

I run a groggy diagnostics on my other senses.

Hearing. The hushed roar of tires negotiating a road beneath. The repetition of a cheesy chorus on an eighties radio station. The wheeze of an air conditioner that has long needed attention.

Smell. The wispy scent of Mom's perfume. The pine-tree air freshener forever dangling from the rearview. The conditioned leather of her car.

Touch. The seat belt cutting into my neck at an angle I'll pay for later. The sweat on the back of my legs, pasting me to the leather.

Road trip.

I used to love this about my parents. I'd come home from school and the car would already be packed. We'd take off without a destination, me and Mom and Dad and sometimes my best friend, Chloe. Just driving and seeing and stopping when we wanted to see more. Museums and national parks and little specialty stores that sold things like plaster castings of Sasquatch footprints. We fell victim to Dad's hobby as an amateur photographer, forced to hold touristy poses for the camera and the sake of memories. To this day, our house is practically wallpapered with past road trips—pictures of us giving one another bunny ears or crossing our eyes and sticking out our tongues like asylum patients.

The car jolts, sending my thoughts chasing after each other in a hazy race. Memories churn in a kind of mental whirlwind, and a few clear images pause and magnify themselves, like still-life photos of a normal day. Mom, doing dishes. Chloe, smiling at me. Dad, sitting at the kitchen table. Galen, leaving through the back door.

Wait. Galen . . .

All the images line up, filing themselves in order, speeding up, animating the still shots into a movie of my life. A movie that shows how I came to be buckled in Mom's car, groggy and confused. That's when I realize that this is not a McIntosh family road trip. It couldn't be.

Two and a half years have passed since my dad died of cancer.

Three months have passed since the shark killed Chloe in

the waters of Destin. Which means that three months have passed since I met Galen on that beach.

And I'm not sure how much time has passed since Galen and his best friend, Toraf, left my house to retrieve Grom. Grom, the Triton king, Galen's older brother. Grom, who was supposed to mate with my mother. Grom, who is a Syrena, a man-fish. A man-fish who was supposed to mate with my mother. My mother, who is also Nalia, the long-lost supposed-to-be-dead Poseidon princess who's been living on land all these years because _____.

Speaking of Her Esteemed Majesty Mom . . . she's lost her freaking mind.

And I've been kidnapped.

2

GALEN STEALS glances at Grom as they approach the Jersey Shore. He looks for emotion on Grom's face, maybe a glint of happiness or gratitude or excitement. Some hint of reassurance that he made the right decision in bringing his brother here. Some sign of encouragement that he didn't completely unravel the cord of his life by telling Grom where he's been. Who he's been with. And why.

But as usual, Grom is like a stingy oyster, all rigid exterior and sealed shut, protecting everything inside. And as usual, Galen has no idea how to shuck him. Even now, as they reach the shallow water, Grom floats like an emotionless piece of driftwood making its inevitable journey toward shore.

Galen retrieves a pair of swimming trunks bunched up under a familiar rock—one of the many hiding places he has around Emma's house—and hands them to Grom. He leaves his brother to stare at the Hawaiian-style fabric while he and

Toraf find their own pairs of shorts and slide them on. Before Galen switches to human form, he takes the time to stretch his fin, kneading his fists into the length of it. Ever since they left Triton territory, his fin has ached nonstop because of all the tension leading up to this, up to Grom reuniting with Nalia.

Up to the answers they've all been waiting for.

Finally, Grom changes to human form and eases the trunks up as if the leg holes were lined with shark teeth. Galen wants to tell him that putting on a pair of shorts is the easy part. Instead, Galen says, "The house is just a short walk up the beach."

Grom nods, tight-lipped, and plucks a piece of seaweed off his nose as his head emerges from the water. Toraf is already on shore, shaking off the excess water like a polar bear. Galen wouldn't be surprised if Toraf broke into a run to get to the house; Galen had insisted on leaving Rayna behind. Given their current standing as outcasts to both kingdoms, Grom was more likely to believe Toraf than either of his own siblings at the moment. Luckily, Yudor had reached him first, and had already informed the Triton king that he himself had sensed Nalia's pulse. Yudor is the trainer of all Trackers, and Toraf's mentor. There is no arguing with Yudor.

Still, it would have been a lot easier if Nalia would have just accompanied Galen and Toraf to Triton territory. Convincing Grom she was alive was almost as difficult as convincing him to come ashore. But just like Grom, Nalia had closed herself off, unwilling to offer even the slightest explanation for what happened all those years ago. The only words they could finally extract from her were a strangled "Bring Grom to me, then."

Short of dragging her to the water kicking and screaming—and destroying Emma's trust in him—Galen made the snap decision to leave them both in Rayna's care. And the word "care" can be very subjective where his sister is concerned.

But they couldn't waste any more time; with Yudor's head start on them, a search party might have already been dispatched, and if not, then Galen knew it was coming. And he couldn't—wouldn't—risk them finding Emma. Beautiful, stubborn Half-Breed Emma.

And he's a little perturbed that Nalia would.

The three of them plod holes in the sand reaching up to Emma's back porch, alongside a recent trail of someone else's—probably Emma's—footsteps leading from the beach. Galen knows this moment will always be burned into his memory. The moment when his brother, the Triton king, put on human clothes and walked up to a house built by humans, squinting in the broad daylight with eyes unaccustomed to the sun.

What will he say to Nalia? What will he do?

The steps creak under their bare feet. Toraf slides open the glass door and ushers Galen and Grom in. And Galen's heart plummets to his stomach.

Whoever tied Rayna to the bar stool—the same bar stool occupied by Nalia last time he'd seen it—made sure it would be a painful fall if she tried to move too much. Both of her hands are bound behind her with an electrical cord, and each of her ankles are cinched to the stool with a belt. A broad piece of silver tape over her mouth muzzles all the fury bulging in her eyes.

Toraf runs to his mate. "My poor princess, who did this to

you?" he says, tugging gently at a corner of the tape. She snatches her face away from him and chastises him in muffled outrage.

Galen strides to them and promptly rips the tape from Rayna's mouth. She yelps, raking him over with a scalding look. "You did that on purpose!"

Galen wads the tape into a sticky ball then drops it to the floor. "What happened?"

Rayna squares her shoulders. "I'm going to kill Nalia for good this time."

"Okay. But what *happened*?"

"She poisoned me. Or something."

"Triton's trident, Rayna. Just tell me what hap—"

"Nalia kept saying she needed to go to the restroom, so I let her use the downstairs bathroom. I figured it would be okay because she seemed to have calmed down since you left, so I untied her. Anyway, she was taking a long time in there." Rayna points to the bathroom below the stairwell. "So I checked on her. I knocked and knocked but she didn't answer. I opened the door—I should've known something was off since it wasn't locked—and the bathroom was dark. Then she grabs me from behind and puts something over my face. The last thing I remember is Emma standing in the doorway screaming at Nalia. Next thing I know, I wake up in this chair, tied up like some common human."

Toraf finally frees her. She examines the red lines embedded into her wrists. Rubbing them, she winces. "I'm going to do something bad to her. I can be creative, you know." Rayna clutches her stomach. "Uh-oh. I think . . . I think I'm gonna—"

To her credit, she does try to turn away from Toraf, who's now squatting on his haunches to unstrap her feet. But it's as if he were the target all along, as if Rayna's upchuck were attracted to him somehow. "Oh!" she says, vomit dripping down her chin. "I'm sorry." Then she growls, baring her teeth like a piranha. "I hate her."

Toraf wipes the wet chunks from his shoulder and gently lifts Rayna. "Come on, princess," he murmurs. "Let's get you cleaned up." Shifting her in his arms, he turns to Galen in askance.

"Are you serious?" Galen says, incredulous. "We don't have time for that. Did you not hear what she just said? Emma and Nalia are gone."

Toraf scowls. "I know." He turns to Grom. "Just so you know, Highness, I'm upset with Princess Nalia for tying Rayna up like that."

Galen runs a hand through his hair. He knows how this works. Toraf will be useless until Rayna is sufficiently calmed down and happy again. Trying to convince his best friend of doing anything otherwise is a waste of time they don't have. *Unbelievable.* "There's a shower on the third floor," Galen says, nodding toward the stairs. "In Emma's room."

Galen and Grom watch as Toraf disappears up the stairwell with their sister. "Don't worry, princess," they hear him coo. "Emma has all those nice-smelling soaps, remember? And all those pretty dresses you like to wear ..."

Grom cocks his head at Galen.

Galen knows this looks bad. He brings his brother to land

to reunite him with his long-lost love and the long-lost love has tied up his sister and run away.

Not to mention how else this looks: illegal. Rayna wearing human dresses and taking showers with human soaps and up-chucking human food. All evidence that Rayna is much more familiar with the human way of life than she should be.

But Galen can't worry about how anything looks. Emma is missing.

It feels like every nerve in his body is braided around his heart, squeezing until it aches incessantly. He stalks to the kitchen and flings open the garage door. Nalia's car is gone. He grabs the house phone on the wall and dials Emma's cell. It vibrates on the counter—right next to her mother's cell phone. Dread knots in his stomach as he dials Rachel, his human assistant. Loyal, devoted, resourceful Rachel. At the beep he says, "Emma and her mother are gone and I need you to find them." He hangs up and leans against the refrigerator, waiting with the patience of a tsunami. When the phone rings, he snatches at it, almost dropping it. "Hello?"

"Hiya, sweet pea. When you say Emma and her mother are 'gone,' do you mean—"

"I mean we found Rayna tied up in their house and her mother's car is gone."

Rachel sighs. "You should have let me put a GPS tracker on it when I wanted to."

"That's not important right now. Can you find them?"

"I'll be there in ten minutes. Don't do anything stupid."

"Like what?" he says, but she's already hung up.

He turns to Grom, who is holding a picture frame in his hands. His brother traces the outline of Nalia's face with his finger. "How is this possible?" he says softly.

"It's called a photograph," Galen says. "Humans can capture any moment of time in this thing they call a—"

Grom shakes his head. "No. That's not what I mean."

"Oh. What do you mean?"

Grom holds up the picture. It's an up-close black-and-white photo of Nalia's face, probably taken by a professional photographer. "This is Nalia." He runs a hand through his hair, a trait he and Galen inherited from their father. "How is it possible that she's still alive and I'm just now learning of it?"

Galen lets out a breath. He doesn't have an answer. Even if he did, it's not his place to tell his brother. It's Nalia's place. Nalia's responsibility. *And good luck getting it out of her.* "I'm sorry, Grom. But she wouldn't tell us anything."

3

THE MORE I stare at it, the more the popcorn ceiling above me resembles an exquisite mosaic. Yellow rings from a leaky roof add pizazz to the imperfect white mounds; the reflection of a parked car outside the hotel room highlights the design in a brilliant, abstract pattern. I try to find a name for this provocative image and decide on "Cottage Cheese, Glorified."

And that's when it becomes obvious that I'm distracting myself from thinking about the U-turn my life just took. I wonder if Galen is back yet. I wonder what he's thinking. I wonder if Rayna is okay, if she has a killer headache like I do, if chloroform affects a full-blooded Syrena the way it affects humans. I bet that now she really will try to shoot my mom with her harpoon, which reminds me again of the past twenty-four hours of craziness.

The scenes from the previous night replay in my head, a collection of snapshots my memory took between heartbeats:

Beat.

Galen reaching his hands in the dishwater. "You've got a lot of explaining to do, Nalia."

Beat.

A flash of Galen grabbing Mom's sudsy wrist.

Beat.

An image of Mom growling as Galen turns her around in his arms.

Beat.

A still life of Mom flinging her head back, making contact with Galen's forehead.

Beat.

A shot of Galen slamming into the fridge, scattering a lifetime's motley collection of magnets onto the floor.

Beat.

Beat, beat, beat.

The still shots become live action.

Mom attaches to him like static cling, the knife poised midair, ready to fillet him like a cod. I scream. Something big and important sounding shatters behind me. The sound of raining glass drowns me out.

And it's that one second that Galen needs. Distracted, Mom turns her head, giving Galen a breadth of space to dodge the blade. Instead of his flesh, she stabs the blade into the fridge. The knife slips from her soapy hands and clinks to the floor.

Beat . . . Beat.

We all watch it spin, as if what happens next depends on which direction it stops. As if the blade will choose who will make the next move. It feels like an intermission from delirium, a chance for sanity to sneak in and take hold. Ha.

Toraf passes me in a blur, bits of what used to be our bay window sparkling in his hair like sequins. And just like that, sanity retreats like a spooked bird. Toraf tackles my mother and they sprawl onto the linoleum in a sickening melody of wet squeaking and soft grunting. Galen kicks the knife into the hallway then belly flops onto them. The tornadic bundle of legs and arms and feet and hands push farther into the kitchen until only the occasional flailing limb is visible from the living room, where I can't believe I'm still standing.

A spectator in my own life, I watch the supernova of my two worlds colliding: Mom and Galen. Human and Syrena. Poseidon and Triton. But what can I do? Who should I help? Mom, who lied to me for eighteen years, then tried to shank my boyfriend? Galen, who forgot this little thing called "tact" when he accused my mom of being a runaway fish-princess? Toraf, who... what the heck is Toraf doing, anyway? And did he really just sack my mom like an opposing quarterback?

The urgency level for a quick decision elevates to right-freaking-now. I decide that screaming is still best for everyone—it's nonviolent, distracting, and one of the things I'm very, very good at.

I open my mouth, but Rayna beats me to it—only, her scream is much more valuable than mine would have been, because she includes words with it. "Stop it right now, or I'll kill you all!" She pushes past me with a decrepit, rusty harpoon from God-knows-what century, probably pillaged from one of her shipwreck excursions. She waves it at the three of them like a crazed fisherman in a Jaws movie. I hope they don't notice she's got it pointed backward and that if she fires it, she'll skewer our couch and Grandma's first attempt at quilting.

It works. The bare feet and tennis shoes stop scuffling—out of fear or shock, I'm not sure—and Toraf's head appears at the top of the counter. "Princess," he says, breathless. "I told you to stay outside."

"Emma, run!" Mom yells.

Toraf disappears again, followed by a symphony of scraping and knocking and thumping and cussing.

Rayna rolls her eyes at me, grumbling to herself as she stomps into the kitchen. She adjusts the harpoon to a more deadly position, scraping the popcorn ceiling and sending rust and Sheetrock and tetanus flaking onto the floor like dirty snow. Aiming it at the mound of struggling limbs, she says, "One of you is about to die, and right now I don't really care who it is."

Thank God for Rayna. People like Rayna get things done. People like me watch people like Rayna get things done. Then people like me round the corner of the counter as if they helped, as if they didn't stand there and let everyone they love beat the shizzle out of one another.

I peer down at the three of them all tangled up. Crossing my arms, I try to mimic Rayna's impressive rage, but I'm pretty sure my face is only capable of what-the-crap-was-that.

Mom looks up at me, nostrils flaring like moth wings. "Emma, I told you to run," she grinds out before elbowing Toraf in the mouth so hard I think he might swallow a tooth. Then she kicks Galen in the ribs.

He groans, but catches her foot before she can re-up. Toraf spits blood on the linoleum beside him and grabs Mom's arms. She writhes and wriggles, bristling like a trapped badger and cussing like a sailor on crack.

Mom has never been girlie.

Finally she stops, her arms and legs slumping to the floor in defeat. Tears puddle in her eyes. "Let her go," she sobs. "She's got nothing to do with this. She doesn't even know about us. Take me and leave her out of this. I'll do anything."

Which reinforces, right here and now, that my mom is Nalia. Nalia is my mom. Also, holy crap.

"Emma, you can't ignore me forever. Look at me."

This startles me. I pull my gaze from the decrepit ceiling and settle it on my fruitcake mother. "I'm not ignoring you," I tell her, which is the truth. I'm aware of every infinitesimal move she makes. Since I woke up, she's crossed and uncrossed her legs six times while sitting at the mini-table by the door. She's tightened her ponytail eight times. And she's peeked out the window twelve times. I figure it's my duty as a captive to keep tabs on my kidnapper.

Mom crosses her legs again, and leans forward on her forearms, resting her chin on one hand. She looks tired when she says, "We need to talk about all this."

At first, I snort. Then the absurdity of the statement—the *understatement*—really takes hold, and I start to laugh. In fact, I laugh so hard that the headboard taps the wall with each out-of-breath giggle. She lets me go on for a long time, clutching my own stomach, filling and emptying my lungs until I reach a natural pause in my amusement. I wipe away the tears of unjoy before they stain the hideous, stiff bedspread.

Mom starts to shake her leg, which is her sitting-down version of foot tapping. "Are you finished?"

I sit up, rippling the bedspread around me like a flash-frozen lake. The room spins, which is on my top-ten list of unpleasant scenarios. "With what, exactly?"

"I need you to be serious right now."

"Probably you shouldn't have drugged me, then."

She rolls her eyes and waves in dismissal. "It was chloroform. You'll be fine."

"And Rayna?"

She knows what I'm asking, and she nods. "She should be waking up right about now." Mom sits back in her chair. "That girl has the personality of a mako shark."

"Says the nut job who chloroformed her own daughter."

She sighs. "One day you'll understand why I did that. Today is obviously not that day."

"No, no, no," I say, palming the air with the universal "don't even" sign. "You don't get to play the responsible parent card. Let's not forget the little matter of the last eighteen-freaking-years, *Nalia*." There. I said it. This conversation is finally going to happen. I can tell by the expression on her face, by the way her mouth puckers in guilt.

Nalia, the Poseidon princess, folds her hands in her lap with irritating calm. "And it would appear that you've been keeping a few secrets yourself. I'm ready to show and tell, if you are."

I lean back on my elbows. "My secrets are your secrets, remember?"

"No." She shakes her head. "I'm not talking about what you are. I'm talking about who you've been with. And what they've been telling you."

"Galen told you everything before he left to get Grom. You know as much as I do."

"Oh, Emma," she says, her tone saturated with pity. "They're lying. Grom is dead."

This is unexpected. "Why would you think that?"

"Because I killed him."

I feel my eyes get wide. "Um. What?"

"It was an accident, and it was a long time ago. But I'm sure your new friends don't believe that. Galen and Toraf didn't leave to get Grom, Emma. I'm positive they were bringing a Syrena party back to arrest me. Why else would they leave Rayna behind to guard me?"

"Because you were acting like a psycho?"

"If only it were that."

It takes a few minutes to process this and Mom gives me some space from the conversation to do it. Over and over, I repeat to myself that Mom thinks Grom is dead. Like, really and truly believes that he is. Which forces me to reconsider a few things.

I've never actually seen Grom. All I know about him is what Galen told me. Thing is, Galen has lied to me before. My gut somersaults with the realization that he could still be lying. But why would he? To make sure I didn't help Mom escape?

Could Galen and Toraf be so terrible that they would trick me again, in order to have my mother arrested?

On the other hand, I can't forget the fact that my own mother lied to me, too. For eighteen-freaking-years. Then she drugged me, kidnapped me, and planted me in some dumpy motel that smells like 1977. Still, it's the middle of the week, which means I'm missing school and she's missing work. She wouldn't just haul us out of our lives if she didn't think the situation was serious.

More than that, her confession seems to ripen her to old age, to drag down her mouth and eyes and make her whole body sag in the chair. She truly believes Grom is dead.

When she doesn't say anything else, I shrug at her. "Could you please just tell me everything? This whole one-tidbit-at-a-time thing is killing me." Seriously.

"Right. Sorry." She tightens her ponytail for the ninth time. "Okay. Since you know about Grom, I'm assuming you know we were supposed to be mated."

"Yes. And I know about your argument and the mine explosion."

My mother's bottom lip quivers. Mom is not a crier. It's hard to believe that something that happened so long ago still affects her like this. And I kind of resent it, on behalf of my dad. After all, she's mourning another man. Well, mer-man. She doesn't get like this when she talks about my dad, and he's only been dead for a little more than two years now. To her, Grom has been dead for decades.

"Let me guess. They told you Grom lived through the explosion, right?" She's almost shaking with anger. "Well, I'm telling you that he didn't. When I woke up, he was gone. I couldn't sense him anymore."

"That's exactly what Galen said about you. That you were nowhere to be found."

She mulls over this for a minute, then says, "Emma, when a Syrena dies, you can't sense them anymore. Grom and I could sense each other half the world apart, sweetie. We were just . . . connected in that way."

This hurts me. Galen had said Grom and Nalia seemed meant for each other from the very beginning. I thought it was ridiculously romantic. But that was before I knew Nalia and my mother were the same person. *Did she not care about my dad at all?*

"So you didn't even look for him? You just assumed the worst and headed toward land?" Somehow, it makes me feel a little better to say it like that.

"Emma, I didn't sense him—"

"Did you ever stop to think the explosion might have messed up your sensing abilities?" I blurt. "Because Galen said Grom's were screwy for a little while after the explosion. But even the Trackers stopped sensing you."

She blinks at me. Opens her mouth, then closes it. Then her face gets all red, and I can see the proverbial dead bolt slide into place. So much for show-and-tell. "Grom is dead, Emma. Galen used you to get to me."

I fling my legs over the side of the bed. "What do you mean?"

"I mean, Emma, that Galen developed this whole little romance with you to earn your trust, to turn you against me. Galen is a Triton Royal, sweetie. There's no way he would attach himself to . . ."

"A Half-Breed," I say, anger and hurt roiling in my stomach. By Syrena standards, Half-Breeds are abominations. I think of all the kisses, the touches, the tingles that passed between me and Galen. The absolute fire I feel when he simply brushes against me by accident. Could he really be capable of acting that way toward someone he truly loathed? He did lie to me before. Could this be another lie? Did he just change his story to keep me hanging on?

All I can really count on right now is that someone I love is lying to me and there's only one way to find out who it is: get them face-to-face.

I know for a fact that if Galen went through all this trouble in seducing me to get to my mother, he will certainly send his hound dog, Rachel, to sniff us out. Galen will come for us, I'm certain of it. And when he does, he'll either bring Grom with him like he claims, or he'll bring the Syrena party to arrest my mom.

If I let it slip to Mom that he'll give chase, she'll keep on fleeing. She thinks she's in danger and she thinks I'm in danger. She won't ever stop. And somehow, I've got to find a way to bring them together and keep us safe at the same time.

Life just got sucky.

Real tears well in my eyes, but not the kind Mom is hoping for. She nods, misled sympathy etched into her features. "I'm sorry, sweetie. I know you really cared about him."

I nod, too, and force the next words out of my mouth. Words that may or may not be true. "I've been so stupid, Mom. I believed everything he said. I'm sorry I didn't tell you."

Mom gets up from the chair and sits next to me on the bed, pulling me to her with one arm. "Sweetie, you don't have anything to apologize for. It was your first taste of love, and Galen took advantage of you. I'd like to say that's only a Syrena trait, but it could have happened with any human boy, too. I'm here for you. We've got to stick together, you and me."

The sincerity in her voice makes me feel as big as a thimble. Not only is she hurting for herself, and reliving Grom's loss, but she's hurting for me, and what she perceives as my loss of Galen. Whether it really is my loss of Galen remains to be seen, but I let her hold me anyway because I'm not brave enough to look into her eyes. Finally, she says, "I'm going to take a shower and wash the travel off me. Then we'll see about dinner, and make a game plan together. Sound good?"

I nod and she squeezes my shoulder. She smiles the "mother smile" before she goes into the bathroom. When I hear the shower curtain close, I pick up the phone.

Galen's wary voice answers. "Hello?"

"Hi," I tell him, just as wary. In the background I hear a muffled hum and wonder where he is.

He breathes a sigh into the phone. "Emma." The way he says my name hurts me and excites me at the same time. Hurts, because what if Mom's right, and he's using me? Excites, because what if she's wrong, and he really does care about me enough to sound like my calling him completed his life? "What happened?" he says.

Before I can answer, I hear Rayna in the background. "I already told you what happened. Her mother is crazy as a caught fish."

I snicker, but then peek at the bathroom in guilt. Lowering my voice, I say, "Yeah, pretty much. We're at a hotel in . . ."

I fumble through the nightstand drawer as quietly as I can, looking for the usual motel stationery. Picking up the notepad, I tell him, "I'm in Uptown. At the Budget Motel."

"I know," he says. "Rachel tracked you down by your mom's credit card. We're on our way." Of course Rachel found us. Being an ex-mobster makes you a Swiss Army knife of Skills People Shouldn't Know. I just didn't realize she would do it this fast. I won't underestimate her again.

It sounds like Galen covers the phone with his hand. I hear something clink in the bathroom and I shove the notepad back in the drawer. "I don't have a lot of time," I whisper into the phone. "Mom's in the shower, but she'll be out soon." I realize Mom takes short showers, not because she's a busy ER nurse who's eternally on call, but because, like me, she can't enjoy the luxury of hot water. Her Syrena skin is too thick to feel the heat. For her—and for me now—showering is just a matter of hygiene. There is no lingering for enjoyment anymore.

"Galen," I blurt. "Mom thinks Grom is dead. She thinks you're going to arrest her for his murder." I'd meant to keep that a secret until I could see his reaction in person, but the bigger part of me couldn't keep it in. Now I've given him a chance to come up with a good story and make it sound believable. You know, if he's not already telling the truth.

Silence. Then, "Emma, Grom is sitting next to me. He's not dead. Why would she think that?" There's a weirdness to his voice though. Something feels off. Or does it? Am I being hyper-paranoid?

"I don't have time to explain. I think she just turned the shower off."

"Do you think she'd believe it if she talked to him on the phone?"

I think about that for a second. It's possible we could end this madness right now. Put Grom on the phone and have him chitchat with her until she's satisfied it's him. But Mom's so adamant that Galen can't be trusted that she'd probably just write it off as a trick. Then she'd know that I called Galen, and she wouldn't trust me anymore, either. And she'd know Galen has a way of tracking us. The best way is to bring Grom to her in the flesh—if Grom really is alive.

It hurts to have to think in that context. That Galen could be lying and tricking me as well. Which is why physical proof—a walking blob of Grom DNA—is needed. "She won't believe it's him. You have to bring him to us."

He lets out a gust of air into the phone. "Emma, listen to me," he says, and stupidly, I press the phone tighter to my ear. "I need you to stall your mom. We're about two hours away from you. Don't let her take off again."

I roll my eyes. "Yeah, it was stupid of me to let her drug me that last time. Really should have seen that one coming."

I can almost hear Galen grin. "Be good, angelfish. We'll be there soon."

I hang up the phone and stare at it for a couple of seconds, at the dirt crusted around each number. This phone, this decaying hotel room, has probably seen a lot of things in its time. But I doubt it's heard a conversation like that. A conversation in which a fish prince is trying to hunt down a dead fish princess and her half-human daughter using the stealth of an ex-mobster.

"I'd hoped we could trust each other, sweetie."

I startle at Mom, who's standing by the bathroom door, arms crossed. Fully dressed. Fully dry. The shower is still going full blast. She must have heard everything. "You don't know for sure he's lying," I tell her, trying not to visibly gulp.

"Pack up. We're leaving."

"Grom's in the car with Galen." I pick up the phone again and point the earpiece at her. "You could talk to him if you don't believe me."

She walks over to me and takes the phone. She stares at it long enough for the receiver to start an impatient out-of-order buzz. She slams it down on the receiver. "It's just a trick, Emma. Pack up."

"I'm not going."

"Oh, but you are."

It's the first time I realize my mom could probably take me in a tussle. She's full-blooded Syrena. Her bones are harder, her skin ticker, her build more muscular. She fought off Galen and Toraf. Plus, there's this look in her eye right now. A survival-instinct kind of look. A make-the-hard-choice kind of look. And she's already proven to what lengths she'll go to keep me "safe."

It's a weird feeling to size up your mom like this. I decide it's so weird, so unnatural, that I don't give it any more thought. So I can't stall my mom here. The opportunity will present itself again, I'm sure. Some how, some way, I will put her face-to-face with Galen again. And I will find out the truth. I stand.

"They'll find us, you know."

"We'll see about that."

4

GALEN PEERS into the rearview mirror at Rayna and Toraf in the backseat. They're leaned up against each other by their temples, sound asleep. *Must be nice.*

But even if Galen didn't have to drive, he still wouldn't be able to sleep. Not with Grom here. Grom, wearing human clothes. Grom, buckled up in an SUV. Grom, cocking his head slightly toward the speaker in his door, trying to listen to the human music without appearing too interested.

Grom, who hasn't said a single word since they left Emma's house.

"She thinks you're dead," Galen tells his brother without looking at him. "She thinks she killed you. Why would she think that?" Out of the corner of his eye, he sees Grom glance in his direction. Still, he's not expecting it when his brother actually answers.

"She's probably blaming herself. For the explosion."

"So, she came to land because of a guilty conscience?"

"She was always hoarding the blame for things that weren't her fault." Then his brother actually smiles. "Most things *were* her fault, mind you, but even when they weren't, she wanted to keep the blame all to herself." After a moment, he says, "I would have loved to see her tie Rayna up. When she was bent on something, there was very little that ever got in the way of doing it."

This takes Galen by surprise. Up until now, Grom had always struck Galen as . . . well, as old-fashioned. Not that his brother ever had a choice—he was always destined to mate the firstborn third-generation heir of the Poseidon house. It didn't mean he had to enjoy his union with Nalia, but by the looks of it, he was fairly smitten. Which doesn't sound like the Grom Galen knows. Most Syrena males seek out docile females for their mates. It seems that noble Grom had fallen for the exact opposite. Nalia is the definition of feisty. And if she's even a fraction of the feisty that Emma is, then Grom had his hands full all those years ago. And apparently, he liked it that way. *Join the club,* as Rachel always says.

"Was the explosion her fault?" Galen said as an afterthought. He regrets the question as soon as it leaves his mouth. But Grom doesn't seem affected.

"Oh, I'm sure she thinks it was. But it was my fault. *Only* my fault." His brother laughs, a sharp gust that sounds more like disgust than humor. "You know the irony in all this, little brother? The whole reason we were arguing that day was because she wanted to explore land. She had a fascination with humans. And as soon as she opened up to me about it, I took it upon myself to crush her dreams. To protect her."

The silence that follows is noisy with the past, with memories that belong solely to Grom and Nalia. Their last day together. Their last words. The explosion. Galen can tell his brother is reliving the emotions, but still storing the details inside, where he's kept them all these years. It feels like seeing a shipwreck from afar through murky water. The outline is there, the damage is visible. But the specifics of how it sunk, how it came to sit on the bottom of the ocean, are still unknown to all except those who experienced it.

Then all at once, Grom clears the murk. "I refused to explore land with her. But I didn't just stop there. I also forbade her from doing it anymore."

"Anymore?"

"She'd been keeping a supply of human clothes on an island close to land. She changed into them on the island, then took a rowboat to land and actually walked among the humans. She even brought things back to Mother, for her collection of human relics."

Galen's mouth almost drops to his lap. "Mother knew she was breaking the law?"

Grom snorts, then shakes his head. "She knew and encouraged it. You know how she loved her human relics."

Galen did know. She'd left behind an entire cave full of them when she died—and Rayna had picked up where their mother had left off. *Are daughters always so much like their mothers?* Rayna takes after their mother in almost every way. And apparently Emma takes after Nalia in many aspects. For instance, Galen knows forbidding Emma to do anything is the best way to get her to do it. "So that made her angry and she fled from you," Galen says, almost to himself. He imagines Emma doing the exact same thing. And it almost chokes him. "Into the mine."

"Oh, not directly into the mine. She allowed me to chase her all over the territories first. Of course, I could have stopped. I could have let her go, let her calm down for a while. It might have saved us from making such a Royal spectacle. But the look in her eyes did not settle well with me. The disappointment there clearly said I'd failed an important test." Grom adjusts in his seat, so he can face Galen. "And you should know that she didn't set off the explosion in the mines. The humans did. At the time, it seemed humans all over the world were at war with one another, and they brought their disagreement to our territories. They built giant ships that could go underwater instead of skim on top of it."

Galen already knew this. When he'd first told Rachel about what happened and how long ago, she'd researched it for him. According to human history records, Nalia had disappeared in the middle of what came to be called World War II. It was not a good time to be human. He wonders if Nalia knew the condition of the human world at the time before she decided to become part of it.

"But she knew that going ashore with the humans was against the law. She should have known you'd be upset."

Grom raises a brow, taking care to scrutinize his surroundings, starting from the clothes on his own body, to the window and everything outside it, and finally resting his gaze on Galen's hands clutching the steering wheel. "Tell me, brother, how concerned were you about the law when you were so busy amassing such an extensive collection of human things?"

Galen grimaces. "Good point. But you should know that I was always concerned about the law, even if I was breaking it. I still *am* concerned about the law." *Especially about certain aspects of it.*

His brother does not miss his meaning. "The law regarding Half-Breeds has been in place for many centuries, Galen. It is deeply entrenched into the hearts of our kind."

"That's not the answer I was looking for."

"I know."

"I won't be without her."

"I know."

By the look on his face, Grom does know. But what can be done? If there was a way around the Half-Breed law, wouldn't Grom ease his mind by offering the solution? So even though the law is what it is, is Grom giving his unspoken consent for Galen to be with Emma regardless? Or is he given an unspoken command that Galen end his relationship with her?

Galen wants to ask, wants to settle things now before they get any more complicated—and while Grom is in a vulnerable, divulging mood. But Galen hasn't been responsible in looking for road signs since this conversation first started. Even now, another exit—maybe theirs—zooms by them. He's in a bit of awe of human drivers who seem to be able to conduct all sorts of business while driving. Apparently, Galen isn't capable of carrying on a simple conversation while watching for road signs. The worst part is, they *should* be reaching their exit any time now. But then again, Galen hasn't been able to drive the speed limit. Every time he gets up to speed, Grom tenses up and scowls at him until he slows down. *Old people.*

Abruptly, Galen sees their exit and takes it. He slows down to a crawl around the curve, which appears to irritate the driver behind him. But the driver behind him doesn't have hundreds of years left to put up with Grom.

Galen scans the main road for a sign with directions to the Budget Motel; Rachel said Nalia used her credit card to check in there earlier. A wave of excitement courses through Galen when he sees the dilapidated sign. The lights are burnt out behind the *g* and an *m*, and to Galen, it looks like a smile missing some important teeth. The hotel is one story, L-shaped. It looks even more neglected than the sign. Some of the windows have masking tape across them. Other windows have blankets instead of curtains hanging in them. Galen wonders why Nalia would choose such a place.

As they near the entrance, it occurs to him just how crestfallen he was not to find Emma at her house where he'd left her. The churning disappointment of not seeing her when he'd expected to, of not wrapping her in his arms the way he'd planned. He glances at his brother, trying to imagine what exactly it was like for him to lose Nalia all those years ago. If Grom felt for Nalia the way Galen does for Emma, then it must have felt like a living death. Every single day.

He should know that I can't allow a tiny law to separate me from her.

Galen pulls into the dark parking lot of the motel as Toraf and Rayna wake up like twin monsters. "Are we there yet?" Rayna says around a yawn, her words almost indiscernible because of her cracked voice.

Galen nods. He creeps the vehicle past room after room,

holding his breath, paranoid that Nalia could somehow identify the sound of the SUV by the way it crunches gravel beneath the tires. But he could be beeping his horn to the tune of the radio and Nalia couldn't care less. Because Nalia's car isn't here.

Where are they? He grabs his cell and dials Rachel, then waits for her to call back. When she does, Galen tries to extract the frantic out of his voice. "They're not here."

"Oh, she's good," Rachel says. "Hold on, sweet pea. Let me look at something and I'll call you back."

Ten minutes later, she does. "Okay," she says, all business. "She took out some cash at an ATM in Chesterfield about half an hour ago. She definitely knows you're looking for her."

"How can you be sure?"

"Because she's using cash now, sweet pea. She might have even checked into the hotel to throw you off. Cash is harder to trace, and she took out enough to get by for a couple of days if she's careful. If she's smart, she'll get off the interstate, too, and take the back roads to wherever she's going. That's what I would do. Your best bet is to get off the interstate when you get to Chesterfield. Then keep your eyes peeled."

"Peeled?"

Rachel laughs. "Peeled, as in everybody needs to be looking for that car. Gas stations, restaurants, rest stops. She has to stop sometime, and she won't stray too far from the main road, not if she's as smart as I think she is. Still, if she's stupid enough to use her credit cards, or make another withdrawal, I'll let you know."

"We're never going to find them." Galen leans his forehead against the steering wheel. Grom stiffens beside him.

"Sure you will," Rachel says. "Tell you what. I'll fly to Kansas, rent a car, and start working my way back toward you. We'll ferret her out that way."

Galen grins. He's not exactly sure what "ferret" means, but he's seen dolphins use Rachel's technique sometimes to trap fish. They come at them from all sides. "Okay. Thanks."

"No sweat."

As soon as Galen hangs up, Grom is pelting him with questions. "Why aren't they here? What did Rachel say? Is Nalia okay?"

It's weird for Grom to be asking about Rachel. Those were two worlds Galen thought would never have anything in common. But they had something in common all along. Him.

"Whoa," Toraf says. "When'd *he* start talking?"

"I have to relieve myself," Rayna says. "Right now. This place looks nasty. Find a clean gas thingy."

Galen eyes his sister in the rearview. "Since when do you need a human toilet to relieve yourself?" She can—and certainly does when the notion strikes her—squat anywhere for that kind of thing. As much as she loves all things human, some of their customs do not appeal to her impatient side.

She shrugs. "I want some cookies, too. Seems more efficient to just make one stop."

Galen pinches the bridge of his nose. *Nalia owes me. Huge.*

5

THE TOWNS start to look alike. Dilapidated fences, ghostly barns, tiny grocery stores whose one car in the parking lot might belong to the owner. And not a single pay phone. You'd think, with how much other ancient stuff these towns keep around, they'd at least have rescued one obsolete pay phone from extinction.

I'm not even sure why I want to use a pay phone. I still don't have a plan B for how I can get my mom and Galen one-on-one without risking our safety; if Galen is the one lying and he did bring a Syrena party with him, I'd be putting Mom at risk for arrest and me for ... I don't want to think about what they'd do to a Half-Breed like me. And even if I had a plan B for escape, executing plan A—getting them face-to-face—is pretty stinking difficult since Mom knows I already tried to stall her once. There's no way she'd let me get away with it again.

Still, the bigger part of me is not convinced that Galen is

lying. Maybe I'm in denial or whatever, but he seems too real, too open with me to be lying. Not that I think Mom's lying, either. I could tell that she truly believes that she killed Grom and that our lives are in real danger. But it could be that she's mistaken somehow. Maybe Grom really is alive and maybe they really did leave to go get him. Maybe there is another crazy explanation for why they each thought the other was dead for half the century.

The thing is, I can't take the chance. I can't just stand around and keep my mom prisoner with lies when I'm the only one she can really trust. I feel bad about calling Galen. But I feel bad about ditching him, too.

I've just got to figure out how to get to the truth without endangering anyone. And until I do, there's no point in even calling Galen.

Which is good, because obviously it's more important to these townsfolk to salvage things like fire-hazard gas pumps that still have the rolling-dial numbers instead of preserving something more useful, like pay phones.

And at least the interstate had decent fast-food choices. In the backwoods route Mom opted for, we've got to choose between mom-and-pop diners with mismatched tables and hot sauce bottles for toothpick holders, or fast-food chain knockoffs with questionable health standards.

My stomach growls for the eleventh time. With Mom's urgency to put as much distance between us and Galen as possible, I've now skipped breakfast and lunch.

"I'm hungry, too," Mom says without looking at me. "I

think we're just going to have to tough it out at one of these little hole-in-the-wall places." When I roll my eyes, she says, "Remember when we took that road trip to Atlanta, and we found that dumpy little diner right outside the city? You said they had the best peach cobbler in the world. Maybe we could get lucky here." But her expression doesn't look quite as hopeful as she scans the roadside for options.

She chooses a stucco building that boasts "We Serve Breakfast All Day" with a huge sign in the front window. When we open the door, a velvet sash tied to the handle and overwhelmed with jingle bells alerts the five patrons that we've arrived. We take a booth by the front window and Mom orders coffee.

I peer over my menu, watching as she dumps sugar into the steaming cup. It's something I've seen a million times; she's always had a little coffee with her sugar. But I've never seen it knowing who and what she is. Before, she was just Mom with a caffeine addiction. Now, she's Nalia, the Poseidon princess. There is no sugar in the Syrena world. There is no coffee. Galen dry heaves at the first taste of either.

Mom notices me noticing her. "You might as well ask," she says, as if any amount of stirring could dissolve the pound of sugar she's dumped in her cup.

I unroll my silverware. "I was just wondering how long it took you to get used to human food." I eye her cup for emphasis.

"Ah." Just then, the waitress, whose name tag says "Agnes," returns for our order. As if to promote irony, Mom orders pancakes with extra syrup. I get a burger. Restaurants like these usually build a decent burger.

When Agnes leaves, Mom corrals the mug with both hands as if trying to keep it warm. "I don't drink coffee for the taste. But what's not to like about sugar, right?"

"Galen gags on anything sweet. Mostly, he gags on anything not seafood."

Mom smiles, as if she's only tolerating the sound of Galen's name for the sake of talking about sugar. "It takes some time. I've been on land quite a while, Emma." She leans closer, lowers her voice. "Since World War II. If you think about it, that means I've been human longer than I was ever Syrena."

She says this as if I actually know the real date of her birth. My eyes are in danger of falling out of their sockets. I already knew that Syrena live to be hundreds of years old. That they age well. Sure, Mom has a few grays streaking her hair. Some wrinkles tugging at her blue eyes. But she doesn't look like the moldy four years old she's claiming.

She presses her lips together as the waitress sets a bottle of syrup on the table. When she leaves again, Mom says, "That's it? No more questions?"

Oh, but there are. "How did you really meet Dad?" I realize then that I feel a sense of disconnection with my life. That if Mom isn't who I thought she was, then Dad couldn't possibly be, either. The story was always that they met in college and fell in love at first sight. Now that I reflect on it, the whole story sounds like a generic, all-purpose romance. Boring and cliché and BS.

Mom nods, as if I asked the right question. "We met years after I'd come ashore. I was selling souvenirs on the boardwalk in Atlantic City, and at night I worked at a freak show." She grins. "As a mermaid."

I gasp and she laughs. "Oh, not a real one, mind you," she says, eyes full of nostalgia. "They dressed me up in this ridiculous costume with a sequined fin and had me swim around a huge tank and wave at the tourists. The ring leader—Oliver was his name—liked that I could hold my breath for a long time." She shrugs. "It was pretty cheesy, but it was easy money."

"So you weren't in college."

"I wasn't, no." She takes another sip. "Your father was though. He was visiting for spring break. I mugged him."

"You what?"

"You have to understand I didn't make very much money, even with two jobs. It hardly even paid for my food. I couldn't fish, because—"

"You didn't want anyone to sense you in the water." Otherwise, she could have been pretty self-sufficient.

She nods. "So one day I see this group of cocky college students, spending money left and right. Pulling wads of cash out of their pockets to pay for small purchases, like ice cream." She rolls her eyes. "They were flashing it. They wanted people to know they were rich."

"Doesn't mean they wanted people to mug them," I mutter.

Mom shrugs. "No, but they were trying to attract attention from the ladies, so I made sure to act interested. Your dad was one of them. I'd seen him before. He came to the freak show a lot and just sat there and watched me. Boy, did he make me feel uncomfortable. After a while, he got up the guts to ask me on a date, and all I could think was that a free dinner sounded fabulous. He took me to a nice restaurant and a picture show—that's what we called movies back then. Afterward, he insisted on walking me home, but since I didn't have a home to walk to, I made up an address and let him walk me to it. That's when he told me he'd seen me breathing underwater, in the tank."

The waitress interrupts then, setting Mom's pancakes in front of her, and lowering a tower of beef and cheese and bread in front of me. "You all set, then?" Agnes says.

Mom and I nod. "Let me know if you need anything else," Agnes continues. "Lester just pulled a strawberry pie out of the oven, and it'd be downright sinful if you didn't try it." With an awkward wink, she leaves.

"I want strawberry pie," I tell Mom, shaking the ketchup bottle for my fries. "It's the least you could do."

Mom smiles and steals a fry from my plate. "Agreed. Maybe I'll have a piece, too."

I eye her pancakes doubtfully. "So anyway. What do you mean he saw you breathing underwater?"

"Well, you know we draw water into our lungs, and get oxygen from it, right?" She lowers her voice to an almost-whisper.

I nod. Dr. Milligan had told us that, after studying Galen. I wonder if Dad discovered this feature of Syrena lung function while studying Mom.

"I tried to be discreet about doing it, you know, taking small breaths, or going to the opposite side of the tank. But somehow he noticed." She drizzles the pancakes with syrup for what seems like a decade. Then she sets to cutting them up. "Well, that officially ended our date, to say the least. But more than that, it meant I had to leave the boardwalk. I couldn't risk him blowing my cover—though, when I think about it, I'm not sure how he would have proved it—but I didn't have the resources to leave on my own. So I pulled a gun on him and demanded his wallet."

The soda in my mouth becomes the soda in my nose. "You had a gun?" I cough and sputter into my napkin.

Mom's eyes go round and she presses her finger to her lips, mouthing, "Shhh!"

"Where did you get a gun?" I hiss.

"Oliver lent it to me. He was always looking out for me. Told me to shoot first and run. He said the asking-questions-later part was for the police." She grins at my expression. "Does that earn me cool points?"

I swirl a fry in the mound of ketchup on my plate. "You want cool points for pulling a gun on my father?" I say it with all the appropriate disdain and condescension it deserves, but deep down, we both know she gets mega cool points for it.

"Psh." She waves her hand. "I didn't even know whether or not it would fire. And anyway, he didn't hand me his wallet. He propositioned me instead."

"Okay. Ew."

"Not like that, you brat. He said he'd seen my kind once before. In Alaska, swimming under the ice. He never told anyone, because he was sure they wouldn't believe him. He asked if I'd let him study me. He said he was going to school to be a human doctor. He said he'd give me a place to stay, and he'd pay me."

"An exchange. Kind of like Dr. Milligan and Galen."

"Who?"

"Oh," I say. "Dr. Milligan is a marine biologist who works at the Gulfarium in Florida."

Mom raises her brow. "That trip you took to visit Galen's dying grandmother? That was to see Dr. Milligan?"

I nod, not bothering to hide my cringe.

Mom sets her fork down. "Exactly how much does that man know about us?"

"Everything. But you don't need to worry about it. He's known Galen for years."

"Oh?"

I roll my eyes, unwilling to let go of this juicy story in favor of fighting over Galen's trustworthiness. Besides, she's being a hypocrite. She trusted a human—my dad—so why can't Galen trust Dr. Milligan? "So . . . it wasn't love at first sight then? With Dad? You fell in love later?" I don't know why I feel disappointed. I don't even believe in love at first sight. Except where it applies to my parents being perfect for each other. And anyways, isn't that a kind of child-myth that all kids want to believe?

"Sweetie . . . It was never love."

Screw disappointment. Now I feel gut-kicked. "What do you mean? But you had to . . . Then how did I . . . ?"

Mom sighs. "You were . . . the result of a moment of . . . weakness on my part." But she takes too long to choose her words. I wonder what she thought of first, instead of "weakness." Pity? Stupidity? She dabs her napkin at some imaginary syrup at the corner of her mouth. "The only weak moment we ever had, which is kind of extraordinary. Not that I regret it at all," she says quickly. "I wouldn't trade you for anything. You know that, right?"

I wonder if "I wouldn't trade you for anything" is also a child-myth. "So I was an accident. Not even the normal kind of accident. Like, a one-night stand, or a oops-I-didn't-take-mypill accident. I was an oops-I-accidentally-mated-with-my-fish-experiment accident." I put my head in my hands. "Lovely."

"That man loved you, Emma, from the moment you were born. He'd be very upset to hear you talking like that right now. Frankly, I am, too. I was not some experiment."

I bite my lip. "I know. It's just . . . a lot, don't you think?"

"That's why we're going to have two pieces of strawberry pie, Agnes," Mom says, her voice strained.

I pull my stricken face from my hands and force it to smile. "Yes, please," I say. I'm beginning to think Agnes isn't a waitress for financial gain. I think she needs gossip to thrive. There's no way a normal waitress would be or should be this attentive.

"Stop feeling sorry for yourself," Mom chides when Agnes leaves. "Your father and I were very good friends."

"This is so weird." It hurts my feelings on behalf of my dad, which is stupid, because according to Mom, Dad was aware of all this friendship crap. And apparently, he was okay with it. "Did you ever tell Dad about Grom?"

"I told him everything. He always thought I should go back. Try to straighten things out. But after you were born, he changed his mind. He didn't want to risk them keeping me, or finding out about you and coming to get you."

We stop talking then. Maybe because I've met my threshold for mind-blowing information. Maybe because Mom's met her threshold for being vulnerable. Whatever it is, we both seem to realize at the exact same moment that we just actually bonded, and now everything feels awkward, like old times. And that if we stay any longer, there might be some unspoken pressure to bond again.

"We'll take some boxes for the pie and the check, please, whenever you're ready, Agnes."

In a few hours the sun will rise and we'll have been driving for a solid twenty-four hours, only stopping for gas, coffee, or the resulting bathroom breaks. My hands feel like permanent fixtures of the steering wheel. When I finally do get to peel my fingers from it, they'll surely be forever curled in place.

Fog hovers over the road in thin strips that look like layers of gauze floating above it. The rising sun will dispatch all those layers soon. After breakfast, it will be Mom's turn to drive again. I glance at her, dozed off in the passenger seat. Either she's starting to trust me again, or she's got some way of knowing if I steer us off course.

The sad thing is, I *am* trustworthy now. I can't let Galen find us until I'm ready for him to, until I have a plan B all sorted out in the event that he's the one lying. But my trustworthiness has nothing to do with why I might steer us off course. We don't have our cell phones, which means we don't have GPS, which means I should be paying attention to road signs, which means I shouldn't be blinking for more than two seconds at a time like I am.

It's just that this road is so straight and boring with hardly any other cars and I can't turn the radio on because Mom is sleeping and since Mom is sleeping there's no one to talk to and—

Whoa. My eyes must be playing tricks on me.

Did we just pass Rachel?

No, it couldn't be. It wasn't even Rachel's car; Galen just bought her a classy little white BMW. The one that passed was a four-door blue something that Rachel wouldn't be caught dead in. Except, the driver looked like her twin sister. All big hair and red lipstick and matching acrylic nails draped menacingly over the steering wheel.

I adjust the rearview mirror and follow the blue car with my eyes without blinking, until my eyes feel like they've pickled inside my head. Just when I think we're in the clear, just when I think I'm letting my imagination run wild, the blue non-Rachel car stops. Makes a sloppy U-turn. Starts speeding toward us with hazard lights flashing.

Fan-flipping-tastic. I stomp on the gas. "Mom, wake up. We've got a problem."

She startles awake and whips a suspicious glance around as if *I'm* the one who's kidnapped *her*. Nice. "Where are we?"

"I don't know, but Rachel—the woman we told you was Galen's mom—found us. She's behind us in that blue car. What do you want me to do?"

Mom's head jerks around to the back window. She curses under her breath. "Who *is* that woman? How did she find us?"

"She's ex-Mafia." I inhale, like I just admitted I'm ex-Mafia or something. It doesn't help that Mom glares at me as if I just confessed to it, too.

"Seriously, ex-Mafia? Like, *the* Mafia?"

I nod.

"Poseidon's beard," she mutters.

I'm pretty sure I won't get used to my mom using fishy cuss words anytime soon.

"Try to lose her."

"It's a long straight road with hardly any turns."

"Well, speed up!" She pops open the glove compartment. Then pulls out a freaking gun.

"Mom—"

"Don't start. It's just to scare her. Usually all you have to do is show someone that you have a gun and that you're not going to take any crap—"

"Did you hear what I said? She's ex-Mob. Her gun probably eats guns like that for breakfast."

She clicks the gun like a pro and three bullets pop out into her hand. Watching your mother do something like this is surreal—even under the circumstances. "Three," she breathes. "It'll have to do."

Panic closes off my windpipe. "What happened to just showing it to her?"

"Like you said. She's ex-Mob."

"You can't shoot her. You just can't." But she reloads like maybe she can. Suddenly I'm having a hard time staying in my lane on this long, straight road.

"I'm not going to shoot her. I'm just going to shoot *at* her." Then that freaking lunatic rolls down the window. "Besides," she grunts, "if I wanted to kill someone, it would have been Rayna." She hangs her head out and pulls the gun through with her.

Options, options, options. Sometimes options are a luxury. Sometimes there is only one option, and usually that one option sucks. Like this time, for instance.

So, I take my one option and swerve off the road.

I hear the gunshot right before we hit.

6

GROM IS playing a game on Galen's cell phone when it rings. Startled, he drops it as if it burned his hand. Galen laughs before he can stop himself. Grom shoots him a sour look but hands him the phone.

"Hey, Rachel," Galen says, still grinning.

"Where are you?" Her voice sounds shaken—something Galen's never heard before.

"We just passed a town called Freeport. Why?"

"You're close then. Good. I found Emma and her mom."

Relief swirls through him, but he knows better than to trust it. Especially with the way Rachel's voice sounds strained. "Where? Are they with you?"

"Galen." Rachel never calls him Galen, only sweet pea. Even when she's mad at him, she just says it through clenched teeth. Terror stabs him all over.

"What? What is it?"

"They were in a car accident. Her mom . . . I think her mom shot herself." That last part sounded more like a question than a statement.

"What?"

"Yeah, I'm pretty sure she shot herself. In the shoulder. She didn't do it on purpose and I don't think it's life threatening, but I haven't seen it up close yet. There's definitely blood. I didn't think it would be a good idea to call an ambulance because of their . . . background. Unless you think I should."

Galen groans into the phone. *Her mom shot herself.* Calling an ambulance that will take her to a human doctor is a bad idea. According to Dr. Milligan, it's immediately evident that the Syrena bone structure is much different from human's. They can't risk any kind of thorough exam of Nalia, like X-rays or extracting her blood.

What else could possibly go wrong?

"There's something else," Rachel says, making the hairs on his neck stand up.

Galen answers her with an impatient grunt.

"I've been shot, too. I can't drive."

If Galen weren't driving, he'd bang his head on the steering wheel. Hard. "How far away are we from you?"

Rachel's breath is short and fast. It's possibly the worst sound he's ever heard. "About thirty minutes yet."

He's hoping she means it's thirty minutes if he adheres to the posted speed limit. "Emma's mother is a human nurse. Maybe she can help you."

"So far she hasn't come over here. I think she's about to skedaddle."

"Is skedaddling bad?"

"It means she's about to leave again, and I can't follow."

"Try to stall them. I'll be there soon, I swear it."

Galen hangs up and bears down on the gas pedal, ignoring Grom's hand when it clutches his forearm. "Nalia's been hurt, Grom. We need to get to her." To his relief, his brother lets go.

And Galen mashes the pedal to the floor.

7

I WATCH as Rachel hangs up the phone and slumps against her car, sliding down the passenger side door and plopping sloppily into the grass. She presses her hand to her stomach in a way that makes my own stomach twist. Her face is pale, her lips quiver. This is the first time I've ever seen this woman in tears. And I don't like it.

With one hand, Mom drops the hood of our car and claps her hands together to dislodge the miscellaneous car gunk from them. She walks to where I'm standing at the trunk and touches my hand. "See if you can start it now, sweetie. I think the battery cable was just loosed because of the impact." When I don't answer, she follows my gaze to Rachel. "You know she just told them where we are, Emma. We have to go."

I move away from her. "She's hurt. You have to help her."

"We have to get away from here."

"You're a nurse, for God's sake! This is what nurses do. We can't just leave her. You *shot* her."

I start toward Rachel, but Mom grabs my hand. "She has a cell phone. She can call an ambulance if she's hurt badly."

"She'll never do it. She won't risk the interrogation involved with going to a hospital with a gunshot wound. And we don't want that, either. Every cop in the area will be looking for us. She'll tell them about us, so they'll pick us up. Come on, Mom. You know this has to be reported if we do it all 'official.'"

Mom crosses her arms. "It sounds like you've covered for this woman quite a bit."

I stagger backward and nod toward Rachel. "*Help. Her.* At least make sure she'll be okay. " Mom glances at Rachel and back to me. I can tell she's thinking of arguing some more. But I won't budge. "If you don't help her, you'll have to drag me away kicking and screaming. It'll be a fair fight this time. No chloroform advantage." Plus, Mom's got a nick on her arm from when the gun went off after we hit the embankment. It's nothing like a gory gunshot wound you see in the movies—in fact, I'm not sure if it's even a gunshot wound because the hole in her shirt is more like a tear than an actual hole. Maybe she scratched herself on the window when it shattered. There's no chunky flesh flapping in the wind or anything and the blood-stain isn't bigger than a fist—and it seems to have stopped seeping through her shirt. My mom is tough and probably wouldn't show pain if she was actually in any, so I don't know how serious it really is. I remember then that Dr. Milligan had said Syrena blood clots faster than human blood. That Syrena wounds heal faster. Still, shattered glass couldn't cut her thick Syrena skin. *Is she shot after all?*

While I'm studying Mom, she's studying Rachel. She's waging war with herself and it's all over her face:

Leave her.

But Emma will fight.

We have no choice but to leave her.

But Emma will make it difficult.

LEAVE HER.

Finally, she sighs and her face changes from war to resignation. I'm not sure if her conscience weighed more than her flight instinct, or if she just didn't want to scrap with me out in broad daylight for anyone to see.

Together, we walk the ten feet back to Rachel's car. The driver's side door is still ajar and the alerting jingle might just give me an eye twitch. I shut the door before joining my mom and Rachel.

Mom kneels beside her. "You've been shot," she tells Rachel.

"You shot me, you crazy bit—"

"We don't have time for the ER protocol crap, Mom," I cut in. "She knows she's been shot. She's alert. Help. Her."

Mom nods. She looks at Rachel's clenched fist where it's balled against her lower stomach. "I'm sorry I shot you. I need to look at that. Please."

Rachel gives her The Stank Eye. Rachel is very good at The Stank Eye.

"I'm a nurse, remember?" Mom says, her voice dripping with impatience. "I can help you."

Rachel inhales and eases her hand away from her stomach,

but I can't bring myself to look at it so I just watch Mom's face to maybe gauge how bad the wound is. I imagine dark blood and entrails and . . .

"What the . . . ?" Mom gasps. As an ER nurse, Mom's seen a lot of things. But by her expression, she's never seen this. I'm thinking it must be way serious. Also, I'm thinking I might throw up.

Until Rachel slaps a handcuff around Mom's wrist. "I'm sorry, *Nalia*. I hope you understand." Then she clinks the other end of the cuff around her own wrist. I steal a glance at Rachel's very clean, very intact, very non-bloody-entrails T-shirt.

Rachel is a smart woman.

Mom lunges for her, hands aiming for her throat. Rachel pulls some karate-chop-move thing and slams Mom against the door behind her. "Knock it off, hon. I don't want to really hurt you."

"You . . . you told Galen you'd been shot," I stammer. "I heard you tell him that. Why would you lie to him?"

Rachel shrugs. "I *was* shot." She glances down at her feet. There's a good-sized hole near the big toe of her boot, and bit of red staining the edges of it. "And I'd better be able to wear high heels after this, or one of you is going to swim with the fishes." Then she laughs at her own stupid Mob joke.

Mom plops down beside Rachel and leans against the car, too, in obvious surrender. She looks up at me. It's a look brimming with "I told you so." And I already know what she's going to say next. We won't make it very far before someone notices two women handcuffed together. Bathroom breaks will be impossible. *Any* public place will be impossible. I'm guessing Mom didn't anticipate needing a hacksaw on this vacation of ours. But I know what she expects from me now. And that's just too freaking bad. I hold up my hand. "I'm not going without you."

"Emma—"

"Not happening."

"*Emma*—"

"No." I whirl around so I don't have to look at her pleading face. Not to mention I feel guilty now because it's technically my fault that my mom is handcuffed to the world's best manipulator. Mom groans and beats her head against the door. Which means she knows that I'm not going anywhere.

Catching my breath, I lean against the front of the car and focus on the individual blades of grass hedging my flip-flop, trying not to throw up or pass out or both. In the far distance, a vehicle approaches—the first one to witness the scene of our accident. A million explanations run through my mind, but I can't imagine a single scenario that would solve all—or any—of our issues right now.

None of us can risk going to the hospital. Mom technically doesn't qualify as human, so I'm sure we'd get a pretty interesting diagnosis. Rachel is technically supposed to be deceased as of the last ten years or so, and while she probably has a plethora of fake IDs, she's still antsy around cops, which will surely be called to the hospital in the event of a gunshot wound, even if it is just in the foot. And let's not forget that Mom and Rachel are new handcuff buddies. There just isn't an explanation for any of this.

That's when I decide I'm not the one who should do the talking. After all, I didn't kidnap anyone. I didn't shoot anyone.

And I certainly didn't handcuff myself to the person who shot me. Besides, both Mom and Rachel are obviously much more skilled at deception than I'll ever be.

"If someone pulls over to help us, one of you is explaining all this," I inform them. "You'll probably want to figure it out fast, because here comes a car."

But the car comes and goes without even slowing. In fact, a lot of cars come and go, and if the situation weren't so strange and if I weren't so thankful that they didn't actually stop, I'd be forced to reexamine what the world is coming to, not helping strangers in an accident. Then it occurs to me that maybe the passersby don't realize it's the scene of an accident. Mom's car is in the ditch, but the ditch might be steep enough to hide it. It's possible that no one can even see Rachel and Mom from the side of the road. Still, I *am* standing at the front of Rachel's car. An innocent-looking teenage girl just loitering for fun in the middle of nowhere and no one cares to stop? Seriously?

Just as I decide that people suck, a vehicle coming from the opposite direction slows and pulls up a few feet behind us. It's not a good Samaritan traveler pulling over to see what he or she can do to inadvertently complicate things. It's not an ambulance. It's not a state trooper. If only we could be so lucky. But, nope, it's way worse.

Because it's Galen's SUV.

From where I stand, I can see him looking at me from behind the wheel. His face is stricken and tired and relieved and pained. I want to want to want to believe the look in his eyes right now. The look that clearly says he's found what he's looking for, in more ways than one.

Then Toraf opens the passenger side door . . . *Wait. That's not Toraf.*

I've never seen this man before, yet he's eerily familiar. His silhouette sitting next to Galen was definitely classic Syrena male, but the glare from the sun had hidden his face. I'd naturally just assumed that where there's a Galen, there's a Toraf. Now that his face is in full view though, I see that this man looks like a slightly older version of Galen. Slightly older as in slightly more jaded. Other than that, he could be his twin brother. It may be because he's wearing some of Galen's clothes, a wrinkled brown polo shirt and plaid shorts. But he shares other things, too, besides clothes.

He's handsome like Galen, with the same strong jaw and the same eyebrow shape and the way he's wearing the same expression on his face that Galen is—that he's found what he's been looking for. Only, the stranger's expression clearly divulges that he's been looking for a lot longer than Galen has—and this man is not looking at *me.*

And that's when I know just exactly who he is. That's when I believe the look in Galen's eyes. That he didn't lie to me, that he loves me. Because this man has to be Grom.

Mom confirms it with a half cry, half growl. "No. No. It can't be." Even if she weren't handcuffed to Rachel right now, I'm not sure she'd actually be able to move. Disbelief has a special way of paralyzing you.

With every step the man takes toward Rachel's car, he shakes his head more vigorously. It's like he's deliberately taking his time, drinking in the moment, or maybe he just can't believe this moment is actually happening. *Yep, disbelief is a cruel hag.*

Still, this moment belongs to the two of them, Mom and this handsome stranger. He reaches the passenger side door and stares down at her with steely violet eyes—down at my mother who never cries, down at my mother who's now bawling like a spanked child—his face contorted in a rainbow of so many emotions, some that I can't even name.

Then Grom the Triton king sinks to his knees in front of her, and a single tear spills down his face. "Nalia," he whispers.

And then my mother slaps him. It's not the kind of slap you get for talking back. It's not the kind of punch she dealt Galen and Toraf in our kitchen. It's the kind of slap a woman gives a man when he's hurt her deeply.

And Grom accepts it with grace.

"I looked for you," she shouts, even though he's inches from her.

Slowly, as if in a show of peace, he takes the hand that slapped him and sandwiches it between his own. He seems to revel in the feel of her touch. His face is pure tenderness, his voice like a massage to the nerves. "And I looked for you."

"Your pulse was gone," she insists. By now she chokes back sobs between words. She's fighting for control. I've never seen my mother fight for control.

"As was yours." I realize Grom knows what *not* to say, what *not* to do to provoke her. He is the complete opposite of her, or maybe just a completion of her.

Her eyes focus on his wrist, and tears slip down her face, leaving faint trails of mascara on her cheeks. He smiles and slowly pulls his hand away. I think he's going to show her the bracelet he's wearing, but instead he rips it off his wrist and holds it out for her inspection. From where I'm standing it looks like a single black ball tied to some sort of string. By my mom's expression, this black ball has meaning. So much meaning that I think she's forgotten to breathe. "My pearl," she whispers. "I thought I'd lost it."

He encloses it in her hand. "This isn't your pearl, love. That one was lost in the explosion with you. For almost an entire season, I scoured the oyster beds, looking for another one that would do. I don't know why, but I thought maybe if I found another perfect pearl, I would somehow find you, too. When I found this though, it didn't bring me the peace I'd hoped for. But I couldn't bring myself to discard it. I've worn it on my wrist ever since."

This is all it takes for my mom to throw herself into his arms, bringing Rachel partially with her. Even so, it's probably the most moving moment I've ever encountered in my eighteen years.

Or at least it would be, if my mom weren't clinging to a man who is not my dad.

I'd rather be in the adjoining hotel room with Rachel, even if it meant watching television on mute while she sleeps with her bullet-ravaged foot propped up on a pillow. But apparently my presence is needed here. Apparently it's very important to hear Mom and Grom fill each other in on the last who-knows-how-many decades they've been apart. To hear how she's missed him so much and still loves him and thought about him every single day. To hear that he swore he sensed her sometimes, that he thought he was losing his mind, that he visited the human mine daily to grieve her loss, blah blah blah.

Galen happens to be in possession of my favorite pair of arms—his—and most of the time when they're wrapped around me, I feel whole and secure and like my blood has turned into hot sauce running through my veins. I should especially be feeling all melty right now. After all, I'd virtually lost him then gained him back within the cruel space of twenty-four hours. But right now his arm feels like a shackle chaining me to the hotel bed—and not in a good way.

What's worse is that he's doing it on purpose. Every time he feels me tense up, as Mom and Grom exchange mushy sentiments and googly eyes, Galen tightens his hold on me. Which makes me wonder what my face must look like. Does it reveal all the betrayal and hurt and pain I feel inside? Is it obvious that I want to fling myself across the hotel room to where they sit together in one chair, my mom on Grom's lap, wrapped around him like there's no such thing as gravity and she's trying to keep him grounded? How apparent is it that I want to put Grom into a headlock until he goes to sleep, and yell at Mom for not loving Dad or caring that he's dead?

I know Mom and I talked about this at the diner. That it was never love, that it was an arrangement that suited them both and that I was an added one-time bonus to that arrangement. But somehow I just can't believe that Dad wouldn't mind seeing this if he were here. Fine, it wasn't love at first sight for my parents. But how, after all those years together, could it not have been love *at all*?

But maybe my expression isn't as bad as I think it is. Maybe Galen's just really good at reading me. Or maybe he's just being overly mushy himself. He is a tad protective, after all. I glance at

Toraf, who's sitting on the other full-size bed next to Rayna. And Toraf is already looking at me. When our eyes meet, he shakes his head ever so slightly. As if to say, "Don't do it." As if to say, "You really don't want to do it." As if to say, "I know you really want to do it, but I'm asking you not to. As a friend."

I huff, then adjust myself in Galen's death grip. It's not fair that Galen and Toraf silently ask me to accept this. That my mother is putty in Grom's proficient hands. That her temperature barely raised a degree around my dad, yet Grom, within an hour of reunion, has her titanium exterior dissolving like Alka-Seltzer in hot water.

I can't accept it. Won't. Will. Not.

How can she sit here and do this? How can she sit here and tell him how much she's missed him, and that she never stopped loving him, when she had my dad?

And ohmysweetgoodness, did Mom just say she's going back? "Wait, what?" I blurt. "What do you mean, 'I'll call my boss and let him know'? Let him know what?"

Mom gives me a rueful smile, full of motherly pity. "Emma, sweetie, I have to go back. My father—your grandfather—thinks I'm dead. Everyone thinks I'm dead."

"So you're just going to go back to show him you're alive? You're just letting him know where you are, right? In case he wants to visit?"

Her eyes get big, full of charity and understanding and condolence. "Sweetie, now that Grom is . . . I'm Syrena."

But what she's really saying is she belongs with Grom. What she's really saying is that she should have never left. And if she should have never left, then I should have never been born. Is that what she means to say? Or am I seriously freaking out? "What about me?" I whisper. "Where do I belong?"

"With me," my mother and Galen say in unison. They exchange hard glares. Galen locks his jaw.

"I'm her mother," she tells Galen, her voice sharp. "Her place is with me."

"I want her for my mate," Galen says. The admission warms up the space between us with an impossible heat and I want to melt into him. His words, his declaration, cannot be unspoken. And now he's declared it to everyone who matters. It's out there in the open, hanging in the air. He wants me for his mate. Me. Him. Forever. And I'm not sure how I feel about that. How I *should* feel about that.

I've known for some time that he wanted that eventually, but how soon? Before we graduate? Before I go to college? What does it mean to mate with him? He's a Triton prince. His place is with the Syrena, in the ocean. And let's not forget that my place with them is dead—no Half-Breeds allowed. We have so much to talk about before this can even happen, but I feel saying so might make him feel rejected, or embarrass him in front of his older brother, the great Triton king. Or like I'm having second thoughts, and I'm not. Not exactly.

I peer up at him, wanting to see his eyes, to see the promise in them that I heard in his voice.

But he won't look at me. He's not looking at Mom, either. He keeps his iron glare on Grom, unyielding and demanding. But Grom doesn't wither under the weight of it. In fact, he deflects it with an indifferent expression. They are definitely engaging in some sort of battle of will via manly staring contest. I wonder how often they do this, as brothers.

Finally, Grom shakes his head. "She's a Half-Breed, Galen."

Mom's head snaps toward him. "She's my daughter," she says slowly. She pulls herself from his lap and stands over him, hands on hips. *Oh, he's in serious shiznit now.* And I can't help but feel elated about it. "Are you saying my daughter's not good enough for your brother?"

Yeah, Grom, are you? Huh, huh are you?

Grom sighs, the triviality in his expression softening into something else. "Nalia, love—"

"Don't you 'Nalia, love' me." Mom crosses her arms.

"The law hasn't changed," Grom says quietly.

"So that's it?" Mom throws her hands in the air. "What about me? I've been living on land for the last seventy years! I've broken the law, too, remember? I broke it before I ever left."

Grom stands. "How can I forget?"

Mom touches his face, all her previous haughtiness diminished into remorse. "I'm sorry. I know that's why we . . . But I can't let Emma—"

Grom covers Mom's mouth with his giant hand. "For once in your stubborn life, will you let me talk?"

She huffs through his fingers but says nothing else. I blink at the two of them, at the familiarity of it all. The way they know how to handle each other. The way they read each other. The way they act like me and Galen.

And I hate it.

And I hate that I hate it.

After Dad died, I told myself I wouldn't be one of those bratty kids who made it difficult for their single parent to date someone else, or to find love with someone else or whatever. I wouldn't be an obstacle to my mother's happiness. It's just that . . . well, I was operating under the assumption that she loved my dad, that they were made for each other, so she probably wouldn't find anyone else anyway. Now I feel that Grom had intruded on their relationship the entire time. That maybe they could have loved each other if it weren't for him.

And somehow I feel that since Mom and Dad didn't love each other, then I'm less . . . important. That I'm the result of an accident that is still complicating the lives of people I love. I also hate that I'm allowing myself to have a pity party when clearly bigger things than myself are happening.

Feel free to grow up at any time, Emma. Preferably before you push away people you love.

Grom retracts his hand from Mom's mouth, and uses his fingertips to caress her cheek. My new and improved grown-up self tries not to think *Gag me*, but I accidentally think it anyway.

"I was going to say," Grom continues, "that I'm sure your transgression can be forgiven, under the circumstances. But I think we should concentrate on that first. I don't think we should bring Emma up at all. Not yet. Solid food is for mature ones."

I feel Galen relax beside me. He nods up at his brother. "Agreed." Then he looks down at me. "They'll need time to digest all this. Once Nalia explains everything, and enough time has passed for them to accept—"

"There's something else," Grom blurts. He rakes his hand through his hair, something Galen does when he's particularly frustrated. I find my immature self thinking, *I don't want Grom and Galen to be alike,* and then my grown-up self says, *Knock it off.* And then Grom says: "I'm already mated to Paca."

The realization slaps us each in a different way.

Me, with elation.

Galen, with . . . I'm not sure. He hasn't moved.

Mom, with horror.

Toraf, with open-mouth shock that makes him look a bit silly.

Rayna, with "You idiot," she spits. "We told you—"

Grom points at her in the universal watch-yo-self sign. "No, you *didn't* tell me. All you told me was that I shouldn't mate with Paca. That she was a fraud. But you . . ." Grom turns to Galen. "And *you* didn't tell me the truth. I won't take the full blame for this."

I can tell Rayna's all kinds of mad, but Galen cows her with a look. "He's right," he tells his sister. Then he nods up at Grom. "But we didn't *know* the truth—well, not the whole truth— until we got back to shore after you banned us from the territories. We didn't know Nalia was alive, but we should have told you about Emma. But are you so sure you would have listened? Seemed like you'd already made up your mind."

Grom pinches the bridge of his nose. "I don't know. Probably not. But I don't think you understand what all this means." By the way Galen cocks his head, I think Grom is right. In fact, by the way everyone holds their breath and looks at Grom, I think none of us knows what this means.

"It means, little brother," Grom says, his voice full of bitter, "that you're next in line to become Nalia's mate."

Ohmysweetgoodness.

8

EVERYONE IS quiet, as if Grom's words deprive the air of its breathable qualities. Nalia takes her seat in a chair this time, instead of his lap. She stares up at Galen in horror, the same horror you feel when you know something's true but every fiber in your body rebels against it. The same horror saturating Galen right now, threatening to push him over the edge and riot against the idea of it all.

The Law of the Gifts states the firstborn of every third generation from each house must mate. That used to mean Nalia and Grom. When they thought Nalia was dead, there were no Poseidon heirs left for Grom to mate with. Grom was free to choose a different mate, which he did. But now Nalia is back from the dead. And though Galen is younger than Grom, he's still from the same generation—and the next heir in line for the Triton kingship if something were to befall his brother.

This cannot be happening.

"I can't believe our parents wanted more offspring after you," Rayna tells Grom. Even hoarse, she's still able to infuse her irritation in each forced word. "After birthing an idiot like you, I'd never even think about having more—"

"Quiet, Rayna," Emma shouts. Emma has obviously learned how to deal with his sister; Rayna leans back against the headboard of the bed and makes her poutiest face. "He's not finished. Keep going, Grom. We're listening."

Grom folds his hands in front of him. "Keep going with what, Emma?"

"The but," she says.

"The . . . the but?" Grom throws an inquisitive glare to Galen, but he pretends not to notice. There's no point. He's got no idea why Emma's talking about butts.

"You know," Emma says, full of polite and calm. "Galen's in line to become Nalia's mate, *but*. That's where you left off."

"Ah." Grom motions for Toraf to move his legs so he can sit on the bed across from Emma. "I'm afraid I don't have anything to offer after the 'but' this time."

Emma stiffens at Galen's side, and he instinctively tightens his hold on her. He's positive he can feel the makings of a temper tantrum rumbling through her. "Oh. So what you're saying is that you're out of your freaking mind."

Grom crosses his arms. This could be bad.

Emma tugs herself from Galen's grasp and stands. Galen knows he shouldn't have let her free, because she's definitely got tantrum all over her face, but he's too curious to see how Grom will react. After all, Grom fell in love with the very female who pulled a knife on Galen. He figures Grom is due for his own battle.

"Galen is not mating with my mother. My mother is not mating with Galen. So run along to your new bride, and leave us all alone."

Galen hears Rayna whisper, "What's a bride?" but he keeps his eyes on Grom, who takes his time standing up, squaring his shoulders. He's seen Grom do this before. Make himself appear as big as possible by invading the space of whoever he's trying to intimidate. A challenge. This is the part where the other person backs down.

But the other person has never been Emma. She steps *toward* the Triton king. "I couldn't help but notice you're still here," she says.

Grom's face softens into what could be amusement. "You and I don't know each other, little one. But I think we both know I'm not leaving."

"You and I seem to disagree on a lot of points," Emma returns.

"Not as much as you think." Grom smiles down at her. "For instance, we both agree that Galen mating with your mother is the worst possible outcome imaginable."

"Is there a 'but' to this statement?"

"*But*, before this gets out of hand, I think we should attempt to fix things the right way."

"Which is?"

"Which is trying to get my mating with Paca unsealed, to start."

Emma frowns. "Trying? What's to try? You're the king. Call it off."

Galen stands and puts a hand on Emma's shoulder. "It's not that simple. The king can overturn mating bonds for others, but not his own. For that, he has to appeal to the body of Archives. It resembles the checks-and-balance system of some human governments we learned about in school."

"But this isn't a problem," Nalia calls from her seat. "The Archives never go against the wishes of the throne."

"It's a bit more complicated than that," Grom says.

"We're the firstborn heirs," Nalia counters. "There is nothing complicated about that. The law is very plain regarding that particular issue. Even you and I couldn't find a way out of it all those years ago, if you'll recall." Her smile is full of meaning and Galen is almost curious enough to ask. He'd always been told Grom and Nalia loved each other since the first time they met. Apparently, that was not the case, if they were looking for a way out of mating with each other.

Grom scowls. "Paca has proven she has the Gift of Poseidon, love. I'm not sure the Archives would unseal me from one who has the Gift. An argument could be made that it goes against the principle of the law, since the law is in place to produce the Gift."

"And if anyone will make that argument, it will be Jagen," Galen says. "I'm certain he's been planning this union for a very long time. That's why he sent Paca to land to learn the hand signals to control the dolphins. He is a patient enemy."

Rayna laughs, but it sounds more like the bark of a seal. "Yes, hand signals! Paca does *not* have the Gift of Poseidon.

Emma has the Gift of Poseidon. She can show you what it's supposed to look like."

"What?" Grom and Nalia say in unison.

Galen and Emma exchange a look; apparently they'd both forgotten to mention this tiny detail to Grom and Nalia. How could they have overlooked this? *Possibly because we were busy convincing each one the other was alive.* "That's how I found Emma," Galen explains. "Dr. Milligan saw her and recognized what she was and called me. That's why Rayna and I were so confident that Paca was a fraud. We'd already seen the true Gift."

"All those years ago in Grandma's pond," Nalia whispers at Emma. "Those catfish. You must have been calling for help. They must have understood."

When Emma was just four years old, she almost drowned in the pond behind her grandmother's house—except that the fish in the pond noticed her distress and apparently pushed her to the surface. Emma tried to explain this to her parents, but her mother never believed her. Until today. Of course Nalia knows what the Gift of Poseidon is. And by the look on her face, she needs no further proof that Emma has it.

"I'm so sorry I didn't believe you," Nalia says. "It never occurred to me that—"

Emma shrugs. "It's over now. We have bigger things to worry about."

"Why didn't you tell me in the diner, when we were spilling our guts about everything?"

"I didn't think you'd believe me. You were so convinced that Galen was lying and just trying to trick us, that I thought mentioning the Gift wouldn't matter to you. That you'd think it was part of the ruse."

Nalia nods. "I'll believe you from now on. No matter what. I promise. I'm so sorry, sweetie."

This time a juicy tear does manage to spill down Emma's cheek, but she quickly wipes it away. Galen fights the urge to pull her to him. "Let's just get on with this."

He knows she doesn't feel as nonchalant as she's letting on. She's been harboring some resentment about the whole thing since she was a small child—for her to let it go this easily seems unlikely. When she gives him a tight-lipped smile, he's certain they'll discuss her true feelings later. He winks at her.

"I'm afraid I don't understand," Grom says. "How is it possible that Emma has the Gift of Poseidon? Her father was human. The Gift can only be produced when—"

"The law is wrong," Nalia says. It seems as if even the walls of the room stiffen with her accusation. "The Gift is genetic."

Galen is suddenly glad that Nalia has been a nurse to humans all these years. She would know how to explain all of Dr. Milligan's logic in a way that Grom would understand. It's not that the principle of genetics is foreign to the Syrena, it's just that humans have taken their study of the subject a bit further—and he's not sure his brother will grasp it.

"Genetic?" Grom says.

"It means that traits from parents are passed down to their fingerlings," Nalia says. "Traits like the shape of their noses, the way they swim, things like that. We already know fingerlings inherit these traits from their parents. But obviously the Gifts of the Generals are also passed down through genetics. Emma is proof of that."

"Then why bother with all the restrictions on the Royals?" Grom asks, unconvinced. "If the Gift can be passed to anyone through their parents, like noses and fins, then why require the Royals to make a sacrifice every third generation?"

"I've thought about that," Galen says. "I'm not sure if the Generals knew about genetics. But if they did, I think they had an ulterior motive for the mating tradition. The arrangement is obviously meant to keep the Syrena united. Having both houses come together every third generation is a way to force us to rely on each other. Instead of the humans."

Nalia nods. "I would have to agree. Emma's father and I discussed it several times. That thought had crossed our minds as well."

Grom looks at Galen. "Is there anything *else* I should know? Anything at all?"

Galen feels it's a bit hypocritical of his brother to point an accusing finger at him. After all, Grom did travel half the big land with him in the search for Emma and Nalia without once mentioning that he'd already been sealed to Paca.

Galen shakes his head. "I think that about covers it. What about you? Do you and Paca have any fingerlings on the way we should know about? Anything that could make this even more interesting?"

"Fingerlings?" Nalia sputters. "Grom, tell me you didn't—"

"We didn't," Grom says. "Triton's trident, there was no time for that, now was there? Galen and Toraf arrived right after the ceremony. Before we left for the island."

"Well, what am I supposed to think? You've gone and mated yourself to—"

"*Knock it off!*" Emma is standing on the bed now, shoes and all, staring down at the rest of them like they've all been drinking salt water. "Do we have the luxury of arguing about every little thing? Or is this meeting with the Archives kind of a time-sensitive deal?"

Grom nods. "Emma is right. We're wasting time."

"So let's get on with this. Go make the appeal," Emma says. Galen knows she's not overly excited to see her mother mated with Grom. But the only way to ensure that Galen isn't the one to mate with her is to unseal Grom from Paca.

Not that Galen would ever take Nalia as his mate. He'd live on land and eat cheesecake for the rest of his life before that happened. But if there is a way to fix this without breaking any more laws, if there is a way to resolve this without leaving behind his heritage, Galen is in favor of at least trying.

Grom takes Emma's hand in his and guides her back to the floor. Galen can tell she wants to recoil, but he's proud of her when she doesn't. He can only imagine what could be going through her mind right now, seeing the intimacy between Grom and Nalia. Even he is surprised by his brother's sentimental behavior toward Nalia. Galen wonders if he's getting a glimpse of Grom's youth, of how he used to be before Nalia "died."

Grom smiles down at Emma. "There is a matter you and I need to discuss, little one. Your mother would have to come with me. She will need to be present to prove that I have a basis for the unsealing. To prove that she's alive. And I want to make sure that is agreeable to you."

Galen sucks in a breath. Emma couldn't possibly know the significance of what Grom is doing. It's more than asking for her permission. More than taking into consideration her feelings. More, even, than respecting her opinion or whatever argument she could propose. This is not for Emma's benefit at all. In doing all these things, Grom is showing Galen—and Nalia—that he approves of Emma. That her Half-Breed status is not something detestable to him personally. That his opinion, even as Triton king, does not necessarily agree with the law.

Which is no small thing, in Galen's eyes. It gives him true hope that someday he will have Emma without betraying everything he's ever known.

Galen glances at Nalia. She's watching Grom and Emma with eyes brimming in tears. Nalia knows, too. She knows what Grom is saying between words.

Emma swallows. "The thing is, I don't understand why any of this matters. Why is this even a discussion? Galen and Mom don't want to mate with each other, so they won't. They don't ever have to go back. They could all stay all land. Even . . . even *you* could."

Grom nods, thoughtful. Galen recognizes his brother's diplomatic expression. "That's true, Emma. I can't force them back into the water, and I wouldn't want it to come to that. And I think we all know there's not much your mother can be forced to do." Grom glances pointedly at Nalia, his eyes full of meaning. "But if I know anything about *my brother*, it's that he's loyal to his kind. To our legacy. If I know him at all, he'll want to at least try to do this the right way first. Because he loves *you* enough to go through the trouble of setting things straight."

Grom is more observant than Galen ever gave him credit for. Galen does want to do it the right way. It's not a small thing to give up everything you've ever known. But it's not a small thing to give up Emma, either. If there is even a slight possibility he can have them both—Emma *and* his heritage—then it's certainly worth fighting for.

The small hope in him swells even bigger.

Grom looks at Galen, an obvious request for support. Galen nods down at her. "I think we should try, angelfish. It would mean a lot to me if we could try."

"And then what?" she says, pulling her hand from Grom's grasp. "Then Grom will mate with Mom and live happily ever after twenty thousand leagues under the sea? And what about you and me, Galen? How's that going to work? What about college and—"

"Emma," Nalia says softly. "These are all decisions that don't need to be made right now. These are all decisions that *shouldn't* be made right now."

Grom nods. "Your mother is right. We need to do what we can now so we have the *freedom* to make these decisions later, when the time comes to make them. Would you not agree, Emma?"

Emma bites her lip. "I guess so."

Nalia stands. "Let's hit the road. I have some arrangements that need to be made before we can leave. I'll change Rachel's bandage before we go. We can set her up in the back of Galen's SUV with some pillows."

9

IT'S ONE of those moments where life seems to pause, and the universe opens its mouth and vomits comprehension on you. It's not knowledge, not cold hard facts that you can talk about in casual conversation, like we did in the motel room, surrounded by Galen and Rayna and Toraf. People who I'd already accepted could sprout a fin. Sure we'd talked about Mom being one of those people, too. But until now, until this, I guess I didn't really believe it.

Even when Galen had stood there in my kitchen and accused my mom of being a dead fish monarch, I thought we'd be having an awkward conversation right now. Maybe trying to explain some inside joke he'd been telling. "You've got a lot of explaining to do, Nalia." Chuckle, chuckle.

Talk is talk is talk. Talk is what we did before true realization hit. Realization that there *had* been an inside joke, and I was the butt of it. For eighteen freaking years. Hardy. Har. Har.

But those were just facts. Knowledge. Like knowing how many feet are in a mile or knowing which city is the capital of China. Facts with no emotion attached. I'd even heard her on the phone a while ago, calling her employer to arrange a leave of absence, paying all the utilities way ahead, droning on about all the things I shouldn't forget to do at the house. It was like planning a vacation or something.

But this? Watching my mom's long silver fin move her through the water behind our house with none of the clumsiness of Natalie McIntosh, the wife-mother-nurse, and every bit the grace and precision you'd expect from Nalia, the long-lost Poseidon princess... This is slap-you-in-the-face comprehension.

And all I can do is watch.

Stretching and twisting, Mom seems relieved to ditch her human legs, the corners of her mouth pulling up in satisfaction. Watching her face, it's easy to believe the transition feels as good as Galen describes. Her tail flits in controlled elegance, in a way that makes Galen's and Rayna's somehow look immature and unseasoned. But the grandeur of the scene seems cheapened by the fact that she's still wearing her tank top—the same one she'd worn on the car ride home, when I still felt, in spite of everything that had happened, that she was just my mom.

She swims toward me now where I wait with my feet anchored into the sand in the shallow water to keep me floating to topside. As she approaches, I study everything about her, taking it all in and trying to process it, but it's her face that gets me more than anything else; she doesn't even have the decency to look apologetic. Guilty would be best, but I'd settle for apologetic. Because she's about to use this tail, this secret extension of herself, this thing she kept hidden from me for eighteen years, to propel herself away, toward the open Atlantic.

And she seems okay with it.

"Surprise," Mom whispers when she reaches me.

"You think?" Of all the anticlimactic ways to begin this farewell. I mean, we're in the water behind the house where I grew up. Where she and my dad deposited me after birth, where she fixed me garbage eggs, where she grounded me for reasons valid and invalid.

She looks down at my legs. "So, you don't have a fin."

I shake my head. This seems to confirm something she already suspected. Her eyes get that serious, listen-to-your-mother glaze in them. "Emma." She grabs my shoulders and pulls me close.

I wrest from her grasp. "I don't hug strangers."

I must sound like a traumatized three-year-old, because Galen darts over to us. Mom waves away a stray piece of seaweed between us and puts her arm around me again. Galen has that look on his face, the one where he intends to drop everything and hold me. Normally that's my favorite look.

But I don't want to be tended to right now. More than that, I don't want anyone to feel the *need* to tend to me right now. I need to keep all these bratty feelings to myself. My dad always told me that holding a grudge is like swallowing poison and expecting the other person to die. I don't want to hold any more grudges. I don't want to swallow poison.

"I know this is a lot to take in," Galen says. He doesn't move to touch me though, which I appreciate.

Grom swims up behind Mom and puts his hands on her

shoulders in a "couple" sort of way and I don't want to, but I hate it, hate it, hate it. I realize I'm going to have to try way harder to embrace my grown-up self. "We won't keep her long, Emma," he says. "We'll be back before you know it. You and Rayna won't even miss us."

"What?" Rayna rasps. "I'm not staying here!"

Grom cuts her a look. "You and your mouth are staying with Emma. It's not open for discussion. This is all going to take a very diplomatic approach, and frankly, diplomacy is not a gift of yours."

Toraf wraps his arms around her from behind. "We need you here, princess. To protect Emma."

She elbows him. "You need me out of the way."

He nuzzles her neck. "You're never in my way."

Galen and Grom exchange an amused look, and I can't help but think they're hypocrites. At any given moment, I could reduce Galen to a cooing mess, and I'm certain my mom would have the same effect on Grom. Galen doesn't miss the reproving look I give him. Before he can explain himself, Toraf cuts him off.

"I sense a party," Toraf says, staring toward the deep. He stiffens, going from Romeo mode to Tracker mode in fast-point-two seconds. "Trackers from both houses. Archives from both houses. All grouped together, moving this way." He looks at Galen and Grom, his eyes full of meaning I don't understand. "I guess they've waited long enough for your return."

Grom nods. "We need to hurry now," he says to Mom.

Mom squeezes me again, eyes full of urgency. Even so, it occurs to me that she is in her true element right now. In Syrena form. Next to the man she has always loved. She is comfortable here in the water. Beautiful. I wonder if the human way of life ever satisfied her. How could it, really? I can't imagine how making coffee, working double shifts, and painting the living room could ever compare to this. To what she has in the water.

"I love you, sweetie," she says. "I'll be back soon." I want to say "Famous last words," but I don't know anyone who's famous, and I don't actually know anyone who's ever said that and not come back. It just seems like one of those classic movie moments where the audience can sense that something bad is about to happen.

And I'm totally picking up on that kind of vibe right now.

As soon as she releases me, Galen grabs my hand and I don't even have time to gasp before he snatches me to the surface and pulls me toward shore, only pausing to dislodge his pair of swimming trunks from under his favorite rock, where he had just moments before taken the time to hide them.

I know the routine and turn away so he can change, but it seems like no time before he hauls me onto the beach and drags me to the sand dunes in front of my house. "What are we doing?" I ask. His legs are longer than mine so for every two of his strides I have to take three, which feels a lot like running.

He stops us in between the dunes. "I'm doing something that is none of anyone else's business." Then he jerks me up against him and crushes his mouth on mine. And I see why he didn't want an audience for this kiss. I wouldn't want an audience for this kiss, either, especially if the audience included my mother. This is our first kiss after he announced that he wanted me for his mate. This kiss holds promises of things to come.

When he pulls away I feel drunk and excited and nervous

and filled with a craving that I'm not sure can ever be satisfied. And Galen looks startled. "Maybe I shouldn't have done that," he says. "That makes it about fifty times harder to leave, I think."

He tucks my head under his chin and I wrap my arms around him until both our breathing returns to normal. I take the time to soak in his scent, his warmth, the hard contours of his—well, his everything. It's really not fair that he has to leave when he's only just gotten back. We didn't have much time to talk on the way back home. We haven't had much time for anything.

"Emma," he murmurs. "The water isn't safe for you right now. Please don't get in it. Please."

"I won't." I really won't. He said please, after all.

He lifts my chin with the crook of his finger. His eyes hold all the gentleness and love in the world, with a pinch of mischief. "And take good notes in calculus, or I'll be forced to cheat off you and for some weird reason that makes me feel guilty."

I wonder what Grom the Triton king would think of that. That Galen basically just stated his intention to keep doing human things.

Galen pushes his lips against my forehead, then disentangles himself from me and leads me back toward the water. My body feels ten degrees cooler when his arms fall, and it's got nothing to do with the temperature outside.

We reach the others just in time to see Rayna all but throw herself at Toraf. I can't help but smile as they kiss. It's like watching Beauty and the Beast. And Toraf's not the Beast.

Then Rayna and I watch as the four fins—our entire

world—swim away from us. When their silhouettes melt into the darker water, my nerves almost riot.

"Do you still sense them?" I ask Rayna. Being half human, my sensing abilities are only half as strong as a full-blooded Syrena.

She rolls her eyes at me.

I decide to do the right thing by not pinching the pure snot out of her. Rayna's under a lot of pressure right now. My mom's arrival to Triton territory will probably cause a frenzy in her kingdom—since Mom's recently resurrected from the dead and all—and Toraf, her mate, will be in that frenzy when it happens. Not to mention she seems to be perpetually saddled with the title of Emma's Babysitter. I know it's killing her to stay behind.

"You think your crazy mother will have another go at it?" she says, turning to me. "Is that why you're asking?" Ahh, so she's still a bit peeved with Mom for all the trouble she's caused. They really do not like each other. "Because fins don't have pockets. It's not like she has all these convenient places to hide another knife."

"My mom wasn't hiding a knife, Rayna. She was *washing* it. Galen took her off guard. He took us both off guard. It was reflex, that's all." I dare her with my eyes to say something else. Besides the withering look she gives me, she keeps her hypocrisy to herself. We both know it's just the sort of crap excuse Toraf makes up for her on a daily basis.

Besides, it really was a reflex. Mom obviously thought I was in danger. And she thought Galen was going to arrest her for being a Syrena deserter. She probably thought all sorts of things in the two seconds it took for her to react to Galen's heavy words: "You've got a lot of explaining to do, Nalia."

I was as surprised as anyone when she pulled the knife from the dishwater and lunged toward Galen with it. So surprised, in fact, that I didn't move a solitary inch from where I stood. Not to help Galen. Not to help my mom. And not to turn the tip of Rayna's harpoon in the right direction so she could at least shoot into the kitchen, instead of impaling an innocent couch.

Maybe Rayna is raw about that. Maybe she thinks I should have helped.

Maybe I should pinch the pure snot out of her after all.

Instead, I ask, "So what happens now?"

She frowns. "Now we wait." Rayna turns toward shore then, moving so slow at first that I think she's waiting for me to catch up. Even against the strong current, I swim my way to her with my puny human legs within a few seconds. But Rayna is not paying attention to me at all. In fact, she's not even swimming. As I pass her, she sags in the water, listless and pliable in the current. Her velvety silver fin, which usually resembles the powerful, ambitious tail of a shark, now looks like a wavering piece of seaweed.

Rayna, who is always so full of grit and spirit and fight. Rayna, who would slap the taste out of my mouth if I said her tail looked like seaweed.

When I reach shore, I can still see her shadow floating just below the surface. And I decide that if Rayna is worried, then so am I.

10

GALEN DOESN'T get truly nervous until he senses the size of the Syrena mass coming toward them. Up until this point, he'd been worried about Emma. What she thought about all this. Her mother's reunion with Grom. What she planned to do while they were gone. Whether or not she was going to keep her promise and stay out of the water.

And . . . his thoughts keep wandering back to their kiss between the sand dunes. It was an exquisite torture, the way she tasted like a mixture of salt water and herself. A combination of two things he's come to cherish. Water *and* land. Syrena world *and* human world. Love for his kind *and* love for Emma.

Only now, as the party of Syrena approaches, its presence seems to encroach on Galen's options. For some reason, it feels like a choice between water *or* land, Syrena world *or* human world, love for his kind *or* love for Emma. According to the law, there never was a choice. But that was before Emma.

And Galen has the feeling that the time for truly deciding between the two is closing in on him. *But haven't I already made that decision?*

He steals a glance at Toraf, who's been wearing the same grim expression since they left Emma's house. Toraf is never grim. Since they were fingerlings, he's always had a special talent for finding the positive in a situation, and if not the positive, then he can certainly find mischief in a situation.

But not now. Now he's keeping to himself. Toraf never keeps to himself. Even Grom, the usual sealed-up clam, has become boisterous and enlivened while he and Nalia chatter to each other, laughing and whispering and holding hands, all the while speculating over the events that separated them so long ago.

But Toraf seems oblivious to the chatter and to Galen's internal war of emotions and to the swarm of jellyfish he just narrowly avoided. Galen had thought Toraf might have been anxious about leaving Rayna behind. Usually, though, he comforts himself by talking about her until Galen wishes he'd had a twin brother instead of a twin sister.

No, what's troubling Toraf has nothing to do with leaving Rayna behind. He even persuaded her to stay. Which means he thinks it's safer for her on land right now. Toraf's motives are always simple: do what's best for Rayna, in spite of Rayna.

From what Galen can sense, there are at least fifty Syrena approaching them; some Galen recognizes, some he doesn't. He knows that Toraf, as a Tracker, has sensed and recognized each one since they stepped foot in the water behind Emma's house. He knew the exact moment they formed a group and began to move in the general direction of the Jersey Shore. And from that exact moment, Toraf has been un-Toraf.

Which makes Galen feel caught in a fisherman's net. Unprotected, powerless, defensive.

All at once, the Syrena party comes into view. And Galen sees the reason behind Toraf's distress. Yudor, the Tracker trainer, leads the group, while Romul and Jagen swim slightly behind him. Together. Shoulder to shoulder.

Galen had suspected that Romul had been helping Jagen secure his place—Paca's place—within the Royal lines. Now he's sure of it. Romul hardly ever leaves the confines of the Cave of Memories. In fact, Galen can't remember the last time he did.

Of course, this *would* be a monumental occasion, what with the return of the Poseidon princess. But there is nothing welcoming or celebratory about Romul's expression. Just indifference, carefully arranged humility, and a bit of scrutiny.

Jagen takes no care to hide his displeasure with the approaching party of Royals. This is, of course, a great inconvenience to him. But for however condescending Jagen appears, his daughter Paca seems to own the appropriate instincts for the situation. She peeks out from behind Jagen, her face full of the kind of apprehension a fraud should be feeling right now.

What bothers Galen the most is not the obvious conspiracy passing between his old Archive mentor, Romul, and Jagen. What is more concerning are the Trackers. And the fact that they've come *armed*. They carry the traditional Syrena hunting weapons—whale bones carved into spears and tipped with angry-looking stingray barbs. These spears have always been used for protection against sharks and ill-tempered squid.

But there are no sharks or ill-tempered squid close by.

So it startles Galen when Grom swims forward to meet with Romul, hauling Nalia with him by the hand. Does he not sense a danger here? *Of course not. Look at him.* Grom appears half crazed with happiness as he pushes Nalia ahead of him and, all at once, presents her to Jagen and Romul.

But before anyone can say anything, before the tension even has time to thaw, a distant cry ripples thought the water. "Nalia!"

Galen doesn't recognize the voice and he's certainly never sensed this older one approaching them. Still, there is a familiarity to him that Galen can't quite place. Something in his facial features, something in his graceful glide. Galen glances at Toraf—if anyone recognizes this stranger it would be Toraf—and is surprised to find that his friend is bowing low as the striking gray-headed Syrena approaches. The others follow suit, dividing into a row of respectful bows as he passes without acknowledging them.

That's when Galen realizes who he is. And he bows as well.

"Father!" Nalia throws herself into his arms and he embraces her fiercely.

Then, in front of everyone, King Antonis of the Poseidon Royals sobs into his daughter's hair. It's a sound full of agony and pain and wonder. "Poseidon's beard, you've come back to me! My beautiful pearl." He squeezes her even tighter. "You've come back."

Galen studies his brother as his brother studies father and

daughter. Grom's smile is full of the kind of peace that results from having everything you've ever wanted. From wrongs being righted, from an overbearing weight being lifted.

From love.

Galen has the feeling that Grom's newborn peace is a bit premature.

Romul proves him right. "Your Majesty, King Antonis, what a great honor to see you after so many seasons! What brings you out of the Royal caverns this day?"

Antonis laughs his surprise. "Romul, I had no idea of your sense of humor, old friend."

"Forgive me, Highness." Romul nods, a counterfeit smile curving his lips. "While I do wish to please you, I'm not entirely sure what I have said that so amuses you, Majesty."

Galen feels his throat constricting. He glances at Toraf, whose jaw has become taut with clenched teeth. Something is wrong.

"Romul, surely you jest. Or has your sight left you in your old age? Even so, surely your sensing abilities haven't failed you." Antonis chuckles and turns Nalia to face the Archive. Nalia smiles widely at him. Galen's gut churns. None of them see what is happening here. "My daughter, Nalia, has returned to us!" Antonis says, squeezing her shoulder.

Romul arranges his demeanor into a sickening graciousness. "Esteemed One, I'm not entirely sure of your meaning. Are you suggesting that this"—he gestures to Nalia—"is the long-dead Poseidon princess?"

Antonis laughs again. *He still doesn't understand.* "Oh, Romul, you clownfish. Of course I'm not *suggesting* it. This *is* my daughter, and clearly, old friend, she is not dead." He sweeps his hand over her in emphasis.

Grom swims up next to Antonis and Nalia. "I'm rather curious to know what *you* are suggesting, Romul." It occurs to Galen then that the Syrena "welcoming" party had not bowed in reverence when they'd first arrived. They'd shown a complete lack of regard for Grom as Triton king.

This time Romul inclines his head, but it's still not the full bow that is customary when first greeting a Royal. "My apologies, my king. I'm not sure where the confusion has arisen, but we will get this matter straightened out, I assure you."

"What matter?" Grom nearly growls.

Jagen swims forward. "The matter of the identity of your guest, of course, Highness."

Yudor fills up the space between Jagen and Romul. "With much respect, I've already confirmed her identity. This *is* Nalia, the Poseidon princess."

Jagen nods. "We do appreciate your involvement, Yudor. You are a much-respected Tracker. And of course, if this were Nalia, you could not imagine our great elation at having the princess returned to us. But you see, other Trackers—Trackers whom you yourself have trained—are convinced that our new guest could not possibly be Nalia. In fact, they have never sensed this newcomer before."

It takes all of Galen's self-control not to wrap his hands around Jagen's throat. He knew something was amiss, but he never saw *this* coming. Grom's unsealing from Paca could have been a simple matter. Until this. Now with Nalia's identity conveniently in question, the Archives have no reason to unseal the union.

We have all underestimated the extent of Jagen's power. And now we'll pay for it.

"I'm not sure which Trackers have told you this," Antonis cuts in, "but they are mistaken."

"Mistaken" is a generous word, in Galen's opinion. "Bribed" would be more appropriate. Or at the very least, "manipulated." Whatever the case, Jagen has been very thorough in his endeavor for power. While Galen was chasing Emma and her mother across the big land, Jagen was apparently adjusting his strategy for the change in circumstances.

Jagen's sigh is full of false sympathy and a hint of cheerfulness. "I'm afraid, Your Highness, we'll have to hold a tribunal to get this all cleared up. But not to worry. I'm sure we can come to a satisfying explanation very soon."

The word "tribunal" seems to contaminate the water between them. Antonis snarls. "I hardly think there is a need for a tribunal. If anyone would recognize her pulse, it would be me. Unless you are questioning my word?"

Romul's eyes grow wide. "Oh no, Esteemed One, not your word. Our intention is merely to discern the truth, to make sure you are not . . . mistaken. After all, you are not actually a Tracker, trained with the memory of pulses, and much time has passed since your daughter—"

Romul isn't the only one startled when Grom surges to within an inch of his face. "I don't know what an Archive might hope to gain from becoming involved with these antics," Grom says quietly. "But I can assure you, I will protect what's mine."

Romul blinks, sways backward. "Yes, please do, Highness. Her Majesty Paca has been awaiting your safe return. It is only fair that you two enjoy some . . . private time with her before we convene the tribunal."

With this, Jagen shoves Paca toward Grom. But she never touches him.

Because Nalia slams into her first.

11

IT'S BEEN two days since Galen and company left, and Rayna's voice has not come back. Which is both a blessing and a curse. On the one hand, she's irritable and anxious and probably doesn't have anything nice to say. On the other, I'm lonely, so even if we were bickering, I'd welcome the distraction.

Rachel has been mothering me and Rayna to death. Even though she's got a broken toe, Mom set her up with one of those air-cast things so she hobbles around the house cooking and cleaning and probably sharpening her knives and polishing her Chinese throwing stars or something. I don't know if she's one of those people who stays insanely busy to keep from thinking about things, or if she just has adult-onset ADD, but whatever the case, she's become overwhelming. Even Rayna thinks so.

"Why can't I go to school with you?" Rayna whispers, but her normal voice comes through the rasp only sometimes, so it sounds like she's undergoing puberty. "If Galen can do it then I can. I'm smarter than him."

I haven't even had the chance to put my backpack down and we're having this argument again. We talked about this fifty-six times already. I know she's anxious and needs a distraction and watching television will only hold in her bottled-up tantrum for so long. But taking her to school is *so* not a good idea. She already caused a scene with the repairmen who came to fix the shattered-by-Toraf bay window in my living room yesterday. Sure, she tried to whisper, but whispering, among many other things, isn't her specialty, and *especially* not now that she sounds like she's yodeling every sentence. But the glass installation guy did not appreciate her remark—which, in her defense, she *had* been trying to *privately* yodel to me—that his nose resembled a lobster claw. "A big one."

I can only imagine what kind of damage she would cause at school. She doesn't know how to play things cool like Galen. Her brain doesn't have that "inappropriate" filter, either. After all, that's why she was left behind in the first place. If she's not fit for the Syrena world right now, I'm not risking exposing her to the human world.

Oh sure, she looks innocent enough right now, surfing the channels on the humongloid flat screen above the fireplace. But I remember not too long ago that there was a *different* flat screen hanging on the wall—and that it had to be replaced with the current one because she picked a fight with me that ended with a literal storm unfurling in the living room and damaging everything.

Rachel shuffles to Rayna and snatches the remote from her. Turning off the television, she says, "I think we should take a trip."

"I have school," I say. "My guidance counselor is already breathing down my neck about my attendance. Besides, I'm tired of traveling." Understatement of the century.

"I don't want to go anywhere in case Toraf—in case anyone comes back for me," Rayna protests.

"Then why are you begging to go to school with me?"

She shrugs. "Rachel would come get me if they came back. But if we all leave, then there'll be no one to come get me."

Rachel crosses her arms. "Well, here's the thing, my little queens. I'm going nuts sitting here waiting to see what happens and I think you are, too. Besides, tomorrow's Friday and it just so happens that they've invented these things called airplanes that can take you anywhere in no time flat."

Rayna perks up. "You mean we get to *fly* somewhere?"

"Where?" I whine. "I'm not exactly in the mood for Disney World and I doubt your foot could—"

"I think it's high time I met Dr. Milligan," Rachel says, raising her chin slightly. "I could use a day or two of room service and at the very least, Dr. Milligan could take a look at Rayna's throat."

"Really? We can fly there?" Rayna looks at me, her eyes full of all kinds of excited. "I've been in the water and been on land, but I've never *flown* before."

I remember the effect flying had on Galen—projectile puking, anyone?—and I'm not really in the mood to be cleaning up Rayna's brand of upchuck. Still, she has this desperate look about her that I can't find it in my heart to ignore. "Fine." I sigh. "You can have the window seat."

Rayna claps like a seal as Rachel walks back to the kitchen. "I'll book the flights for tomorrow after you get home from school. No layovers though. I'm not walking all over the airport with a bum leg."

Rayna bites her lip. "What if someone comes back for us while we're gone?"

"Toraf has a cell phone here and knows how to use it, sweetie," Rachel calls over her shoulder. "No sweat."

Rayna does not get sick on planes. Also, Rayna does not stop talking on planes. By the time we land at Okaloosa Regional Airport, I'm wondering if I've spoken as many words in my entire life as she did on the plane. With no layovers, it was the longest forty-five minutes of my whole freaking existence.

I can tell Rachel's nerves are also fringed. She orders an SUV limo—Rachel never does anything small—to pick us up and insists that Rayna try the complimentary champagne. I'm fairly certain it's the first alcoholic beverage Rayna's ever had, and by the time we reach the hotel on the beach, I'm all the way certain.

As Rayna snores in the seat across from me, Rachel checks us into the hotel and has our bags taken to our room. "Do you want to head over to the Gulfarium now?" she asks. "Or, uh, rest up a bit and wait for Rayna to wake up?"

This is an important decision. Personally, I'm not tired at all and would love to see a liquored-up Rayna negotiate the stairs at the Gulfarium. But I'd feel a certain guilt if she hit her hard head on a wooden rail or something and then we'd have to pay the Gulfarium for the damages her thick skull would surely cause. Plus, I'd have to suffer a reproving look from Dr. Milligan, which might actually hurt my feelings because he reminds me a bit of my dad.

So, I decide to do the right thing. "Let's rest for a while and let her snap out of it. I'll call Dr. Milligan and let him know we've checked in."

Two hours later, Sleeping Beast wakes up and we head to see Dr. Milligan. Rayna is particularly grouchy when hungover—can you even get hungover from drinking champagne?—so she's not terribly inclined to be nice to the security guard who lets us in. She mutters something under her breath—thank God she doesn't have a real voice—and pushes past him like the spoiled Royalty she is.

I'm just about aggravated beyond redemption—until we see Dr. Milligan in a new exhibit of stingrays. He coos and murmurs as if they're a litter of puppies in the tank begging to play with him. When he notices our arrival he smiles, and it feels like a coconut slushy on a sweltering day and it almost makes up for the crap I've been put through these past few days.

Dr. Milligan looks past me and smiles twice as wide. "You must be the famous Rachel, who Galen speaks so highly of."

Rachel laughs. No, the woman *giggles* and she all but waltzes with an air cast up to Dr. Milligan and extends her hand to him. "Famous? Or infamous?"

That's when Rayna and I exchange eye rolls. If this isn't insta-attraction, I don't know what is. And why, why, why I think of it this way I'm not sure, but since Dr. Milligan sort of reminds me of my dad, then this insta-googly-eye thing reminds me of Grom and my mother and how they were drawn to each other like magnets. So in a way, it's like my dad—only it's not really my dad, of course—has found someone else to keep him company. And I don't know how I feel about it.

Which is pretty stupid, since this is Dr. Milligan and Rachel and it's not my business to feel anything about it at all. Also, I should probably grow up soon or I'm going to go freaking crazy.

"Oh, no," Dr. Milligan continues, oblivious to my internal tantrum. "Definitely famous. He adores you, you know."

This is when Rayna pinches me. "What's your problem?" she hisses. Rayna is more observant than I thought. I do not like that Rayna is more observant than I thought.

But I don't have to answer because Dr. Milligan and Rachel snap out of it and try to tend to me just like Galen and Mom did. *This has got to stop.*

"Oh, my dear Emma, are you all right? You do look a bit peaked," Dr. Milligan sings.

I wave him off. "I'm fine. Just happy to be here again. Do you still have Lucky?" Lucky is the beached dolphin the Gulfarium rescued this summer. I like to think I'd bonded with him the last time I was here.

"Of course. We wouldn't release him without allowing you a proper good-bye."

We make our way to the dolphin tank and for some reason I'm nervous about seeing Lucky again. I hope he remembers me. At the same time I realize it would crush me if he didn't, I also realize that I'm getting more emotional by the second. It's like everything in life has become a symbol somehow and I'm reading too much into it.

Grow up, grow up, grow up.

I do grow up, right before I reach my hand into the tank. Lucky remembers me, nuzzling me with his cute little nose. "Did you miss me?" I ask him. And I swear that dolphin nods.

"I missed you, too," I tell him. "Have you learned any new tricks while I was away?"

It turns out Lucky has adapted a bit better since our last meeting. Last time he was sad and homesick, it seemed. This time he seems . . . he seems at home. Before I can allow myself to search for the symbolism in that, Lucky presents me with a soccer ball.

"Emma, do you want to come with us when Dr. Milligan examines Rayna?" Rachel asks. I don't miss her meaning.

I pet Lucky. "I'll be back, Lucky. Then we'll play."

As I pass Rachel to go back down the steps, she pulls me aside. "Is that for real? That dolphin understands what you're saying? Seriously?"

Dr. Milligan chuckles. "Oh, this is going to be fun."

Rayna tugs on his arm. "But me first," she rasps.

"Of course, my dear. Of course. Rachel, won't you join us in the examination room?"

"Goodness, child." Dr. Milligan unclicks the pen light. "Your tonsils are so swollen."

"Is that good?" Rayna asks.

"I'm afraid not. Your vocal cords could be damaged. Has this sort of thing ever happened before?"

Rayna genuinely thinks for a moment. "I'm not sure what you mean by vocal cords, but I lost my voice once when I yelled at Toraf. But it wasn't this bad and it didn't last this long," she croaks. "Can you fix me?"

Dr. Milligan cocks his head. "I'm not sure. Have you been screaming at Toraf recently? You know you're quite hard on him at times."

"Did Galen tell you that? It's just his opinion, you know."

"Galen has mentioned it a time or two." He taps her chin, coaxing her to open her mouth again. Good thing Rachel told her to pop some mints before we came. "Hmmmm," he says. "There seems to be a tear at the top of your mouth. No, not a tear really. It's too . . . *neat* to be a tear. It's more like a hole. A perfect hole has opened up in your mouth. I'm quite certain it wasn't there before." He clicks off the pen light, thoughtful. "Do you know what it reminds me of?"

Rayna shakes her head, eyes wide.

"It reminds me of the hole whales use to make sound. Tell me something, Rayna dear. Does it hurt?"

"What do you mean?"

"Does it hurt to try to talk, for instance? Does it hurt when you don't try to talk? Do you remember what you were doing when you lost your voice?"

Rayna crosses her arms. "No, it doesn't hurt. I just can't talk, I can only whisper. I mean, I think I'm talking normal, but only a whisper comes out instead. And, yes, I *do* remember what I was doing when I lost it. Oh yes I do. I *had* been screaming, just not at Toraf. But screaming doesn't hurt. It usually makes me feel better, actually. Except—" Then she all but accuses me with her eyes.

Oh, lovely. But I guess if anyone should be explaining it, it should be me. "My mom . . . My mom used chloroform on her. To knock her out." I could have put it delicately and fancied it up for Dr. Milligan's sake, but secretly I wanted to see the horror on his face. Not.

"I . . . I see. And how . . . how did she 'use' the chloroform on her?" There are a million other questions on his face, too, but Dr. Milligan is a patient, sequential-order type of person.

"Same way she used it on me, I guess," I tell him. "She put a rag over our faces until we fell asleep." I pause, wait for the shock to subside on his face. "Do you think the chloroform burned a hole in her mouth maybe?"

"Hmm. No, I don't think so. The tissues around it aren't damaged. It appears to be a natural development."

"Does Galen have a hole like this?" Rayna says.

Dr. Milligan purses his lips. "I've recently examined Galen, and he does not have a hole there. Why do you ask? Did he lose his voice as well?"

Rayna does not like this answer. "I wish. But I was thinking that maybe he would have one, too, since we're twins and all."

Dr. Milligan chuckles. "This is one thing you don't share, dear. You get to be the special twin."

"Special means different," she says.

Welcome to the Freak Club, I want to tell her. But because it looks like she's genuinely distressed, not to mention hungover still, I give her a break. There will be plenty of time later to use this against her in an argument. After all, she's lightning quick to call me a dirty Half-Breed.

"Will my voice come back?" Rayna says.

"I think so," Dr. Milligan says. "In fact, I can't really see why this hole would be affecting your ability to vocalize as it is. Just to be safe though, I think you should refrain from talking as much as possible. Just until the swelling goes down. I can give you some anitbiotics for that, too, in case you have an underlying infection I'm not seeing."

"Will anti-buttocks close up the hole?"

Dr. Milligan gives her a smile brimming with pity. "I'm afraid not."

Awkwardness creeps into the room and spreads like a vapor. We're all thinking our own thoughts, and we're all staring at Rayna while we do it.

Apparently Dr. Milligan's thoughts get the better of him. "Emma, why on *earth* would your mother chloroform yourself and Rayna?"

Rachel fluffs her hair and pulls it to one side in a very Italian, very flirty way. "Oh, Dr. Milligan. Have we got some juicy gossip for you."

12

THE POSEIDON Trackers bow to Galen as he passes them at the entrance of the cave. He nods an acknowledgment and continues on his way. When he reaches Nalia's chamber, the two Triton Trackers keeping guard move to block him from entering. *Everyone has gone mad. Six months ago, a Tracker wouldn't dare stall him from going anywhere.*

Besides all that, he wonders what Emma would say if she found out he allowed her mother to be imprisoned in her own territory. But Grom and Antonis both agree that this is best, to show cooperation and to show respect for the traditions of the Law. That being inconvenienced now is for the greater good later.

Galen is not entirely convinced that any greater good looms in their future.

Galen holds up the string of dead fish in his hand. "I've come to give Her Majesty food."

"The newcomer is well fed, Highness. She is not in need of more food."

Galen shakes his head. Before, no one would have dared to deny his request. Not to mention that these Trackers are too young to even know whether Nalia is a newcomer or the true Poseidon heir. Like Galen, they were born after she disappeared and therefore have never sensed her until her reappearance.

Which means they are relying upon information told to them. *Fed* to them by Jagen and Romul. *Grom is right. Solid food is for mature ones. Not young fools like these.*

Under the circumstances, Galen cannot afford to be charitable to insolent tadpoles. To show any kind of weakness right now would be a mistake. Cooperation, yes. Weakness, no. The questions Jagen and Romul have raised delve deeper than the identity of Nalia. They are questioning whether or not the Royals can be trusted. Whether or not the Royals are fit to rule.

Galen makes what Emma calls his "or else" face. "I'm not asking, Tracker. Move aside."

This seems to unnerve the young guard. His face falls. "We . . . We were told to allow no visitors, Highness, aside from King Antonis."

"Antonis or Grom has forbidden me to visit? I find that unlikely." He dares them with his eyes to name Jagen or Romul. They get the point: Royals are still Royals. Royals are still to be obeyed. The Trackers move aside and bow.

Galen finds Nalia gliding along the cavern walls, muttering to herself. Though he knows she's sensed him for some time, and maybe even heard his conversation with the Trackers, she only looks up when Galen speaks. "I've brought you some fish," he says.

She crosses her arms. "Why hasn't Grom come for me?"

Galen steals a quick glance back at the guards. "Surely you remember attacking his new mate?" He's certain that if she had her human legs, she would stomp her foot at that moment. But Grom is doing the right thing. Keeping the peace, and showing objectivity by allowing Nalia to be detained until her identity is decided upon. As far as everyone is concerned, she is a new-comer who has assaulted the Triton queen. Until she is proven to be the Poseidon heir, Jagen has announced her a threat to his daughter's safety.

This is why Galen is glad the throne has fallen to Grom. If Emma were imprisoned, he'd have already gone mad, done something drastic and reckless. If things get worse, he still might. Grom is still too euphoric to see the depths of what is happening here. Antonis, too, it seems.

Galen's heart aches for them both.

"Stop calling her his mate. And she's lucky she brought that many protectors with her. And she's lucky I didn't have my lionfish—"

Galen holds out the fish again. "You should really eat." Right now what Nalia says is treason. Paca is still a Triton queen at the moment. Everything she says can be used against her at the tribunal. And Galen has no doubt the Trackers outside have been instructed to listen intently.

She turns away from him. "I'm not hungry."

"Highness," he says sternly. "Sulking will not help anything.

Eat. This. Fish. It will give you strength. It's a gift from Grom. He says these are your favorite."

She whirls on him. "Cod? He knows I hate . . . Oh." She eyes the fish more closely, notices the point protruding from the last cod's tail. "Oh. Yes, I do enjoy cod." Nalia relieves Galen of the gift. He hopes she understands that she's only to use it if things go badly with the tribunal. A last-resort kind of thing, in case Jagen's influence is more than Grom anticipated, and as much as Galen dreads it is.

The lionfish spike is imbedded into the last cod. Galen wonders that she feels comfortable carrying it at all—lionfish venom is deadly—but Grom insists she'll know how to handle the thing. Grom is not who Galen thought he was all this time. And neither is Nalia.

"He asks that you only eat them if you have to, Majesty." Which sounds so ridiculous that Galen shrugs at Nalia when she rolls her eyes. The guards don't seem to notice the lack of sense in the conversation. But it does appear Nalia understands his meaning.

The tribunal starts tomorrow. The decision would normally be left up to a group of Commons who volunteer for the duty, but since the matter involves Royals, the jury will be made up of a mixture of Archives from both houses. Galen can't recall ever hearing of such a thing, a tribunal being held for a Royal. But since Nalia's identity is apparently still in question, *and* she attacked the current Triton queen in front of so many witnesses, the tribunal will also function as a trial. If Jagen is as smart as Galen is starting to think he is, he already has the verdict tucked neatly into his capable hands.

Her identity will not be confirmed. And she'll be found guilty of treason.

If that happens, she'll be imprisoned in the Ice Caverns until she takes her last breath. And Emma will never speak to him again. He might as well accompany Nalia to the Ice Caverns. The Ice Caverns are more vast than any human prison, and considerably less populated—the Archives estimate that only forty or so Syrena have ever done something grave enough to be sentenced there. It would be a boring, lonely life—and death.

Of course, Galen is hoping that Grom and Antonis will not allow that kind of outcome. He's not sure what kind of alternate plan the two kings have conjured up, if anything at all, but surely for all the desperation he sees in their eyes, they're hiding something more useful than despair behind their anxious expressions. Doing this all the right way is one thing. But there might not be a right way, with Jagen's influence marring the judgment of the Syrena.

Surely, if the right way fails, the two kings will not watch Nalia be imprisoned.

Grom would not suffer all those years only to lose her to the Ice Caverns. But going against the decision of the tribunal would be . . . Galen doesn't want to think of the consequences of that right now. Too much is at stake, not only for Grom and Nalia, but for Galen and Emma as well. If the Archives won't allow Grom and Nalia to unite, the possibility of Galen and Emma ever mating under Syrena tradition is all but obliterated.

The tribunal has to return a positive solution. It just has to.

And if it doesn't? Galen can't fathom what Jagen could possibly hope to gain if the Royals were displaced. *The kingdoms?* Hardly. The Syrena version of a kingdom differs greatly from the human version. When humans say the word "kingdom," they mean palaces, mansions, wealth, people. When Syrena say the word "kingdom," they mean endless strips of ocean. Fish. Reefs. Caverns. The Syrena do not need gold or jewels or paper money for their wealth. The only wealth the Syrena boast of are one another. They trade services sometimes, but mostly they help one another in times of need. They take care of their elderly and young ones.

So then, the only benefit of controlling the kingdoms is to change their way of life. *But what would he possibly change?*

Galen nods at Nalia, who has apparently been watching him think things through. He wonders what she saw in his expression. "I've got to get back now," he says. She shrugs.

Get back to what? he thinks to himself as he leaves her chamber. He's already roamed through the tunnels of the Cave of Memories twice, and each time he's found himself back at the ruins of Tartessos, at the wall where he first figured out that Emma was a Half-Breed. The wall where he's unable to take his eyes off the picture of the Half-Breed girl whose curves remind him of Emma.

Instead of returning there to torture himself, Galen decides to seek out Toraf. His friend has still not pulled himself from his gloomy trance, so at the very least, they could be miserable together. Toraf is close enough to sense, but Galen hesitates. Paca is near as well, and in the same direction he'd need to go to reach Toraf. He's not particularly in the mood for a run-in with the fraud queen.

Still, he has an almost-urgent need to mull things over with Toraf. To miss Emma and Rayna with Toraf. Simmer with Toraf in mutual lovesick misery and anxiety and insecurity.

So when he gets within earshot, he's not expecting to hear Toraf and Paca laughing. Together. Not just a polite laugh, either. They are enjoying, genuinely enjoying, a moment together. A private moment.

A private genuine moment that makes Galen ball his fists. *What is he doing?*

They stop laughing when he reaches them. "I hope I'm not interrupting something," Galen says sourly.

"Of course you're interrupting," Toraf says, slapping him on the back. "It's what you do best, Highness."

Paca giggles. Galen has never seen her like this. Almost at ease, completely natural, instead of uptight like she always is around her father. Completely natural—except for the fact that she still claims to possess the Gift of Poseidon.

"Toraf was just reenacting his recent run-in with a fleet of stingrays. I never realized how entertaining your friend is, Galen." Paca touches Toraf's shoulder in a way that makes Galen think this is not the first conversation that has passed between these two.

"I'd have to agree," Galen says curtly. "He's full of entertaining surprises."

Paca sighs, apparently reminded of the situation at hand. That she's a fraud, that the Royals are on to her, and that they intend to extricate her from the Triton king and her claim to the throne. "I'm afraid I have to leave now. My father is expecting me." Without further explanation, she swirls away.

Galen waits until she's out of sight before turning on Toraf. "What was that about? Were you actually *flirting* with Paca?"

Toraf shrugs. "I'm just trying to make the best of the situation, minnow."

"What could you two possibly have to say to each other?"

"You'd be surprised." Toraf starts to swim away, but Galen catches his shoulder.

"Enlighten me, tadpole. If anyone needs an entertaining distraction, it's me."

They lock eyes with each other. Toraf is definitely hiding something. He's hiding something and he knows that Galen knows he's hiding something. "I'm sure I've already told you about the stingray incident, Galen."

"Toraf."

But his friend shrugs off Galen's hand. "I don't have time for a retelling, Galen. I'm meeting with King Antonis soon and I can't be late."

"Why are you meeting with Antonis?"

"He wants to hear the stingray story, too." Toraf is not a good liar, even when he tries. But right now, Galen can tell he's not even trying. Either he doesn't care that Galen knows he's lying, or he's trying to tell him something with the lie.

Either way, Galen can't figure it out.

"Then maybe I could come and listen to the story." This feels weird, to say things between words with Toraf, his best friend since they were fingerlings learning how to swim straight.

Toraf starts to pull away again. "Sorry, Highness, but His Majesty requested a private meeting."

He never calls me Highness in private. He knows I hate it. Why is he going out of his way to irritate me? Does he sense we're being monitored? Or is this a new Toraf, formal and rigid? Galen watches until his tail disappears into a cloud of krill passing through. And he decides that he doesn't like a formal, rigid Toraf.

So then, there is definitely an alternate plan in the works, and Toraf is part of it and clearly Galen is not.

Which could mean several things. They may not trust him. Why, he couldn't possibly imagine. Or, they could be reasoning among themselves that they're "protecting" him from knowing whatever it is they're planning.

Or worse, they think he would disagree with their plans and try to thwart them.

Which can only mean their plans involve Emma somehow.

13

I RUN the faucet until it's scalding hot, then dump a dab of dish soap into my empty oatmeal bowl to soak. Behind me, I hear Ranya huff as I pick up my backpack. "Why can't I go to school?" she rasps. "Galen went to school. If he could fit in, I could fit in."

Oh, there are so many things I could say to that but Rachel silences me with a look. She walks over to Rayna and squeezes her shoulders. "Oh, sweet pea, you don't want to hang out with those silly humans."

"Yes, I do. *Especially* because they're silly. It's so boring here without—" She straightens up. "It's just boring sitting here watching television all day. I want to *do* something. I can't even get in the water. Toraf will know as soon as I put my toe in."

This surprises me. "I'm not allowed in the water. They never said you couldn't get in."

"Toraf told me not to. He said it was dangerous for me to

get in the water, too. He made me promise on our sealing that I wouldn't."

I put my backpack down and sit on the bar stool next to her. "Dangerous how?"

She shrugs. "He didn't say. But I could tell he was serious."

I don't like this. This new explanation doesn't make sense. In the beginning it made sense to leave Rayna behind because of her fat mouth. It made sense for Galen to ask me to stay out of the water. I'm a Half-Breed. The danger to me is obvious. But Rayna is a Royal. If anything, Royals are the most protected of all Syrena. Theoretically, the safest place for Rayna *is* the water. Or so I'd thought. No wonder she was so listless when they'd left. I wish she had told me this sooner.

I feel my throat closing up. If Toraf thinks Rayna is in danger, does that mean Galen is in danger, too? And what about my mom? Would Galen—would *Grom*—lead my mom into danger?

The biggest obstacle was supposed to be getting Paca and Grom unsealed. Danger was never a factor in all this.

Rachel hands me my backpack, her expression full of meaning. "I'm sure everything is fine. You have the luxury of going to school to keep your mind off things for a while. Be glad. In the meantime, I'll take sweet pea here shopping or something. And I'll try to find you both a distraction for *after* school."

"I'd rather go shopping than to school," I offer, but she pushes me toward the door and hands me the keys to Galen's SUV. Arguing with her is like arguing with Mom. She wins, I lose, and it's usually for the best anyway. I take the keys and go.

~ ~ ~

I don't know how I ever survived school before Galen. Then I realize exactly how—Chloe. There was never an uninteresting day of school with Chloe around. I pass the locker we shared our junior year. The grimy outline of the stickers we slapped all over it still mar it in places. Our initials are still carved in the corner. I wonder if the school decided to leave it that way out of respect because of what happened over the summer. I wonder if after I graduate, they'll clean it up and repaint it. Right now Chloe would be texting me, or walking beside me, or waiting for me at that locker.

But last summer changed all of that. When a shark plucked her from our surfboard and pulled her into the Gulf of Mexico by the leg. Her life ended soon after that. And my life changed. That day marked the first time I used my Gift since I was a small child, though I didn't realize it then—and I certainly didn't realize it while flailing for my life in Granny's pond. It was also the day I met Galen. The first time I sensed him. Really, it was the summer of many firsts.

And now I feel guilty. Have I allowed Galen to replace Chloe? Or worse, have I *used* Galen as a replacement for Chloe? Did I grieve long enough for her? Did I cry hard enough? What if she never died? What if she were still alive? Would there have been room for Galen *and* Chloe in my life? Would they have liked each other, or would I have had to choose between them? And who would I choose? And why do I feel guilty even thinking about who I would choose?

I feel like the person who takes her mind off a headache by stomping on her own toe. I've just exchanged one anxiety for another. Worry about Galen and Mom, or worry about what-ifs over Chloe. It's all the same. It's all worry. I look around the school hall and begrudgingly watch all the kids whose problems amount to homework, getting grounded, or what to wear to prom. Even now, a group of them has gathered around a prom poster, probably discussing how they'll get there, who they're going with, blah blah blah.

This time last year, I'd be standing next to that poster doing the same thing. Chloe and I had decided in the sixth grade that when we got to be seniors, we would go stag (or "stagette," as Chloe called it), even if we both had boyfriends. We declared at the age of eleven that prom was for *us*, not for anyone else, and it would be the best night of our entire existence. Period.

Now that she's gone, I wonder what I should do. Should I uphold that agreement, and go stagette and deprive myself of the sight of Galen in a suit, squirming under the pressure to dance with some kind of grace in front of humans? Or would I even get the chance to go with Galen, given all the things going on right now?

That's when I decide that prom is stupid. It's just a dumb dance that might have meant something to the old me, but the new me doesn't really give a flying frick.

And that's when Mark Baker, whom I now refer to as Galen's BFF because of their testosterone-enhanced run-in last year, walks up to me. "You got your dress picked out for prom? Let me guess. It's violet, to match your eyes."

I raise a brow at him. Since Galen has been gone, Mark has been awfully attentive. Not that Mark isn't nice, and not that if it were a year ago, I'd be a babbling idiot if he took the time out of being godlike to ask what I planned on wearing for prom. But like everything else, Mark is *so* one year ago.

And I don't know if I like that.

I shrug. "I'm probably not going."

Mark is not good at hiding surprise. "You mean Galen won't allow you to——"

"Knock it off. I know you think Galen is controlling or whatever, but you're wrong. And anyways, I can hold my own. If I wanted to go to prom, you can bet your sweet Aspercreme I'd be going."

Mark holds up his hands in surrender. "Simmer down, skillet. I was just asking a polite question. Did you want to talk about starving children or government conspiracy instead?"

I laugh. I'd forgotten how easygoing Mark is. "Sorry. I'm just in a bad mood I guess."

"You think?"

I punch his arm, then feel guilty about how flirty it looks. "Well, nobody's perfect."

The bell rings and he starts walking backward, away from me. "But some people who shall remain nameless are pretty close to it." He winks, then faces the other direction.

Mark is so likeable and good and boy-next-doorish. For a second I fantasize about not being a Half-Breed whose mother is a long-lost mer-monarch and whose boyfriend has a fin or hairy legs, whichever the situation calls for, and whose whole life isn't toppling like a stack of dishes in an earthquake.

I allow myself to think that I am just me, and that Mark is taking me to prom, and that I am going to buy a violet prom dress now because he suggested it, and we will be pronounced prom king and queen and we will dance some of the night and kiss for the rest of it. A small part of me wants it. Not Mark, not exactly. A tiny fraction of me just wants to be *normal*.

But the bigger part of me remembers what my dad taught me about the undertow when he was trying to coax me into the water to teach me how to swim. "If you ever get caught in the undertow," he'd said, "just let it take you. Just let it pull you right out. Whatever you do, don't fight it and waste your energy and oxygen. That's how people die. The people who don't die wait it out. The undertow lets go eventually, right when you think you can't hold your breath any longer. You just have to be patient."

Because right now I'm caught in an undertow. And I've got to hold my breath, be patient, until it gives me my life back.

So I stop thinking about everything in the entire universe and I go to class.

14

THE BOUNDARY has never been so full—at least not as far as Galen can remember. This thin strip of neutral territory runs around the entire earth and is the only place where a tribunal may be held. It reminds Galen of an upright, human version of the equator because it's exactly that—and invisible boundary separating half the world. Syrena from both houses of Royals, and those who crossed over to Jagen's "house"—the house of "Loyals" as they call themselves—cram into the Arena.

The shape of the Arena reminds Galen of the giant bowl Rachel uses for her breakfast cereal. Surrounded by a ring of hot ridges—the humans call them volcanoes—the Arena is a natural valley, flat and boring in contrast to the surrounding landscape. The hot ridges haven't erupted in many years, since before Galen was born. Some of the Archives living today remember stories passed down from older Archives, but no one living today has ever seen an eruption here.

Not to mention, this area is protected by some human law that prohibits fishing here; any time boats or divers come in, some of the humans who live on a nearby island run them off. Very little human activity is ever sighted here. But Galen is certain that if they don't get on with the tribunal, some kind of human technology will detect the activity and investigate—interference or no.

Which, for once, could be a good thing.

So far, Romul has been the only person to give testimony. The old Archive eloquently expressed that he felt the Gift could conceivably pass on to non-Royals under certain circumstances. Galen couldn't agree more—they've already had the genetics discussion. But since Romul isn't familiar with genetics, and he's arguing for the sake of *Paca's* Gift, then Galen can hardly look his one-time mentor in the eye.

As Romul leaves the center witness stone, he says, "And who knows? Perhaps the Royals have . . . strayed in the past. Perhaps Paca has more Royal blood than we suppose?"

The implication is outrageous. More than that, it's treasonous. But Romul is in no danger of being arrested. Right now, the crowd moves as one, alive with whispers. Romul's testimony glides through the water with momentum, building into a wave of shock and awe that cannot be undone. The words are forever imprisoned in their minds, trapped, demanding to be analyzed and picked apart. A hint of distrust will forever taint the relationship between the Archives and the Royals, the Commons and the Royals. Or rather, a hint of distrust will forever just taint the Royals.

Galen looks to Grom, scrutinizing his reaction and finding

next to nothing. His brother is stationed next to Paca, his smiling queen, but it's Nalia with whom he shares his-and-her matching expressions of indifference. Next to the Triton Royals, Toraf clenches and unclenches his jaw, but gives no other outward reaction. Galen's gaze shifts to Antonis, across to the Poseidon side of the Arena. The wizened king looks slightly amused. Of course, after having spent so much time in self-imposed isolation, Galen supposes the king may not know how to act appropriately anymore. Otherwise, he'd have to question His Majesty's sanity in allowing a genuine smirk to tug at the corners of his mouth. As if Romul had told a joke.

Galen wonders what his own expression betrays. Fury? Disbelief? Nervousness? But he's not given much time to contemplate.

Tandel, an Archive from the Triton house and elected leader of the council for this tribunal, takes the center stone and hushes the Arena. "My friends, Romul has given us something to consider, and it is much appreciated. But he is the first to give testimony. If we are to resolve the matter, we must hear from the rest." This seems to placate the masses. Tandel nods in self-satisfaction more than graciousness. "Now, we have Lestar, respected Tracker of House Poseidon, to give testimony."

Lestar is seasoned, of an age to remember Nalia's unique pulse, her identity. Toraf says a Tracker never forgets a pulse. If that's true, Lestar can positively identify Nalia as the Poseidon princess. His testimony, along with Yudor's, will end this ridiculous trial.

To Galen's relief, Lestar wastes no time in doing so. "My friends, thank you for hearing my testimony today. I am honored to be a part of such a happy occasion. Happy because our lost Poseidon heir has returned to us. Many of you older ones are aware that I led the search party after the mine explosion all those seasons ago." This incites nods from among the assembly. Both houses know the story; it's one of the worst tragedies in the history of their kind. "You younger ones have heard the tale passed down through the generations. If you have, you would know that I was one of the last to give up hope of ever finding our princess alive. I searched many days after the last Tracker party was sent out." Lestar turns to Nalia, an affectionate smile pursing his lips. "My friends, please believe when I say this one you call 'newcomer' is not new at all. I swear on the law and my ability as a Tracker, she is Nalia, heir of House Poseidon. I have known this one since the day she released from her mother's belly. Please join me in welcoming her home."

This coaxes a small cheer from some, but mostly a rash of disgruntled moans from the Loyals. Tandel is quick to quiet all, raising both palms toward the crowd.

After a few moments, silence reigns once more. Tandel places a hand on Lestar's shoulder. "Thank you, Lestar, for your fine testimony. We will be happy to take this into consideration as well."

At this, Antonis speaks up. The smirk has vanished from his face. "I wonder that we need to consider further, Tandel. Lestar has just identified my daughter and welcomed her home, as did Yudor upon her arrival. What more is there to say?"

If Galen thought the crowd was silent before, it's speechless now, probably marveling at his mere presence. Antonis has kept himself hidden so many decades. Syrena from both houses seem captivated by his gravelly voice. Galen just hopes that their wonderment isn't keeping them from listening to the king's actual words or to his reasoning.

Tandel recovers with a smile. "Your Majesty, I think I speak for all in attendance when I say how thankful we are that you have honored us with your presence at this tribunal. I do see your point, Highness. But if we are to come to a thorough and satisfying agreement, would it not be wise to listen to all the testimony available to us now?"

Antonis rolls his eyes. "I well know the proper proceedings of a tribunal, Tandel. But she is my daughter. Who else would know her better than I? Why would I bother myself with *honoring* the Boundary with my presence if that were not the case?"

Galen can't help but be amused by Tandel's floundering under the scrutiny of the Poseidon king. He wonders if Antonis was always so blunt and impatient, or if he developed these savory characteristics while isolating himself in his Royal caverns. The king's fit has Toraf grinning like a mischievous fingerling.

"If I may," a voice calls from the crowd. A voice Galen is all-too familiar with. Jagen makes his way to the center stone, and turns to his section of Loyals. He smiles wide and bows before his traitorous followers. "If I may, friends, I would propose a very good reason why His Majesty would claim this stranger as his daughter."

Jagen turns to Antonis, careful to keep the poison in his eyes from infecting his voice when he says, "I propose, friends, that King Antonis would rather claim this newcomer as his daughter and pretend to perpetuate his bloodlines than let his house become useless. You see, if my Paca possesses the Gift of

Poseidon, as many of you have seen already, then what reason do we have for keeping the Royals in so lofty a position among us? King Antonis knows this. If a Common could possess the Gift, then why should we be under the vigilance of Royals, instead of perhaps a leader chosen from among us, one who is more fit to rule?"

Jagen turns to his followers, who cheer with almost violent enthusiasm. Galen feels a knot in his stomach tighten, a knot that grows bigger with each word that spews from Jagen's mouth. Mostly because what he says is true—technically. But Galen wasn't prepared for Jagen to be this blunt, to be this open with his endeavors. And he wasn't prepared for the spirited acceptance of such treason.

No, Jagen didn't name himself as that potential leader. But he didn't have to; he's the one guiding their thoughts, influencing their decisions. It's almost as if he's had this talk with them before, minus the Royals. Jagen had been a very thorough adversary. He continues, "King Antonis has not graced us with his presence nor his leadership for many, many seasons. Only now that his own Royal status is threatened has he bothered to take an interest in our dealings. How can we trust this kind of rulership?"

The Loyals applaud again, but Jagen holds up his hands for silence. "What's more, the Royals think they are above the law. They present us with this newcomer who they say is Nalia, the Poseidon heir. My friends, even if she *were* the Poseidon princess—which will be proven to you she is not—are we to simply overlook the fact that she has been breaking the law for many years, while she claims to have lived on the Big Land among humans? How much longer will we allow the Royals to dilute the law passed down from our esteemed generals?"

The audience roars with mixed emotions. The Arena is almost deafening. And that's *before* Antonis closes his large hand around Jagen's throat.

15

I SET my backpack on the counter and pull a bar stool next to Rayna, who's soaking/drowning a cotton ball in nail polish remover. "I think it's dead now," I tell her.

She gives me a sour look, then proceeds to scrub her big toe like a dirty pot. Rachel sets a glass of ice water down in front of me and a cookie that has nuts, marshmallows, chocolate chips, cinnamon, and . . . I can't tell what else. "What's this?" I ask.

Rachel shrugs. "Dunno. I made up the recipe this morning, but I can't think of a good name for it. I was kinda just craving everything."

I take a bite and all the flavors fight for attention. And I know exactly what to call it. "You should call them Garbage Cookies." I realize how that sounds, and before she can finish her grimace, I say, "No, that's a compliment! Mom makes me garbage eggs all the time. She puts all sorts of stuff in them, like jalapeños, cheese, sour cream, grits." Or at least she *used* to make garbage eggs for me. Before she swam off to play princess.

"Ah," Rachel says. "Well, I don't want to steal your name. How about Dump Cookies?"

"Um. Sure."

"No? How about . . . Upchuck Cookies?"

"Wow. Don't hurt yourself."

She grins. "How about—"

"How about we go check out what Rachel bought us today?" Rayna says, wiping the excess polish remover on a paper towel. She clears her throat in vain. "They're on the beach."

"*They?*"

Rayna nods. "I get the purple one."

I follow her outside and toward the water. It looks like it has rained recently; tiny indents still dot the sand, marking the spot where each little raindrop fell to its death. Where the sand and water meet there are two jet skis, one red, one purple. I stop. "We're not supposed to get in the water."

"You only have to put your foot in to get on. Then you're on top of the water."

"What if I fall off?"

"Don't."

"But—"

"If you're afraid then just say so. Or are you too afraid to *say* you're afraid?" She crosses her arms when I don't budge. "Rachel and I already took them out while you were at school. If you can drive a car, you can ride one of these things."

Not comforting at all, since Rayna can't actually drive. Last time she tried, we assaulted a tree with Galen's little red car and got a free ride home in a cop car. What is Rachel thinking?

I bite my lip and think to myself how Galen would feel if I just stuck my foot in the water, just enough to get on the jet ski. Maybe I wouldn't even have to; maybe Rachel could push me out. Wait . . . "Rachel took this out, bum leg and all, huh?"

Rayna scrunches her face. "Well, she came out and watched me do it. But it's the same thing. She wouldn't do anything she thought Galen wouldn't like."

I step out of my flip-flops and dig my toes in the sand. "I guess not." But even Rachel must have a breaking point, a threshold for tolerating whining. And if trophies were handed out for whining, Rayna would have the biggest.

"He would want you to have some fun, you know," Rayna says sweetly. It's the first time I've ever seen a fish look like a cat. "He would want you to keep your mind busy while he fixes all the little things wrong with the rest of the world."

I decide Rayna is a grade-A manipulator. "He wouldn't want me to risk myself for fun. And he's not trying to fix the world. He's doing what he thinks is best. For us."

"And when is someone going to care what *we* think?" Her words are full of bitter and I wonder if she would have yelled that last part if she had her full voice back. It comes and goes, like a radio station just out of range. Tears threaten to spill through her long lashes. Tears that I'm not sure I can trust.

"What's up with you?" I ask. "Is something wrong?"

She hugs herself as if it's freezing cold out here on the sun-drenched beach. "Yes. No. I don't know. I mean, what's happening? Why hasn't someone come for us? And..." She turns toward the water. "I've been thinking about how your mother lived on land all this time. And how... how I want to live on land, too."

If I keep letting my mouth hang open, my tongue will dry up and shrivel inside my head. Before he'd left, Galen had made his intention of spending more time on land clear. Surely if he could do it, Rayna could do it, too, right? But she's not talking about *more* time on land. She's talking about *all* her time on land. Pretending to be human. Or is she? Is this all part of an elaborate scheme to tug on my heart strings and give in? She already tricked me into teaching her how to drive.

What would Galen want me to do? Would he want me to encourage her to follow the law? Would he want me to encourage her to live on land? And that's when I realize what she's talking about. Scheme or not, I shouldn't encourage her to do *anything*.

Because I'm not her. All she's trying to do is be *her*. At least, that's what I *think* she's trying to do. Now I feel bad for all the crap I give Toraf. You really can't tell when she's playing you and when she's being serious. "You should do what will make you happy," I tell her. "I think we should all do what will make us happy. And if living on land will make you happy, I say go for it."

I can practically see Galen cringe. But Rayna is right. It's time someone asked what she wants. No one asked her if she wanted to stay here and babysit me. No one asked her about mating with Toraf—even though it turned out that she wanted to. What if she hadn't? Would she still be forced? I hate to think so. But I can't convince myself otherwise. Not with this burdensome law the Syrena have clung to for so long.

Sure, there are good things about the law. Galen would argue that same law has kept them safe from humans all these centuries, and he would be right. But I can't help thinking of my grandmother, my dad's mom. She had this crystal figure of a clown holding a bouquet of balloons. I'd only ever seen it once, when she showed it to me while she was cleaning it. As she would turn it over and over in her hands, trying to get to every hidden crevice, it cast a rainbow prism on the ceiling, turning the whole room into a giant kaleidoscope. All the colors danced and played. It was absolutely mesmerizing to a six-year-old. After Grammy had made it shine, she wrapped it up in tissue, put it back in the box, then put the box in the attic. I'd asked why she didn't show it off, put it on display in the house somewhere close to the window, so she could have a ballet of colors on her wall every day. "I want to keep it safe," she'd told me. "I keep it in the box so it doesn't get broken."

That day I learned the exact opposite lesson Grammy was trying to teach me—well, as much as a six-year-old could comprehend of the matter: Grammy's nuts. Also, breathtaking crystal clowns were not made that way for no reason. They were *meant* to be seen.

Now, years later, I can translate that lesson into: safe isn't always better than sorry. Sometimes you need sorry to appreciate the safe. And sometimes safe is just plain boring. Rayna's probably going through a combination of both right now. And who am I to say what's right and what's wrong?

And what is the law to say how she should live?

The law prohibits Half-Breeds. Am I really that bad? The law is like a one-size-fits-all T-shirt. And how often do those shirts really fit everyone?

Rayna studies me, as if she can tell what's going through my mind. No, it looks more like she *planted* what's going through my mind. Suspicion creeps back in.

"Yes, I can decide for myself," she says. "I don't need everyone else telling me how to think or feel about things. I'm a Royal, too. My opinion counts just as much as theirs." She stares down into the water.

This whole time she was making the argument for freedom to live on land. But now I'm not so sure that land had anything to do with it at all. Somehow it sounds like she's saying, "I want to live on land," but meaning something else. Something else, like, "I want to go see what's going on down there."

She strips from her clothes, down to her still-wet bathing suit, and gets a running start for the water. "You're just going to leave me here?" I shout after her.

"I'm not leaving you here, Emma. You're keeping yourself here." She leaves me with those crazy words, and then she's gone.

I am paralyzed on the beach in my school clothes. I can't help but feel that I'm in huge trouble. But why should I? *She* was babysitting *me*, not the other way around, right? It's not like I can chase her down and follow her. Her fins have already gone a distance I can't cover with my puny human legs. Besides, these are my favorite jeans; the salt water would be unforgiving.

Except... There *is* that shiny new jet ski sitting there. I could close the distance between us, put my foot in the water, and find her. She would sense me, come back to see why I was in the water. Wouldn't she? Of course she would. Then I could talk her into staying here, not leaving me alone to drive myself crazy. I could manipulate *her* into feeling sorry for *me*.

Unless she's the complete sociopath I think she is.

Still, it's my only option. I grab the handle to the jet ski and pull it toward the waves. Luckily high tide is coming in and I don't have to drag the thing far. It makes a trail from the beach to the water, evidence that one of us did what we weren't supposed to. Or, maybe Rachel will think that we're riding double. *Yeahfreakingright.* Rachel's specialty is figuring stuff out.

But the more time I spend thinking about all this, the more time Rayna has to put leagues of sea between us. Good thing I don't care about grace as I awkwardly climb aboard and stub my toe. I bite back a yelp, and turn the key in the ignition. The thing roars to life beneath me and all at once I'm one part scared and one part exhilarated.

So, I go.

It's been a few years since I've ridden one of these, and even then I never actually drove one. I piggybacked with Chloe and only after she swore on her little brother's life that she wouldn't do anything reckless. I marvel at how far I've come since then. From scared to get in the water to chitchatting with fish on the ocean floor.

Luckily, my first scream of terror doesn't come until I'm way out of earshot of Rachel, when I think I've grown bored with a lower speed and decide to gun it. The sudden jolt forward almost pitches me off the back end. While my heart rate recovers—along with my pride—I squint into the distance, into the reflection of the setting sun floating like an oil slick on top of the water.

I stare a long time, as if somehow Rayna will give me a sign of where she is if I just keep looking long enough. I let my foot dangle in the water, even as I admit that if Rayna is swimming with any kind of purpose, she's long gone. Behind me the shore is just a flat line with no sign of Galen's house. Not even a speck.

I could turn around.

I *should* turn around.

I twist the handles to turn around.

And out comes my second scream of terror.

The violent thrust of water in my face isn't half as surprising as how loud it is leaving the huge blowhole that has appeared beside me. I cough and sputter and scream again, but this time in frustration. Goliath—my blue whale friend who first convinced me of my Gift of Poseidon—sends another gush of water toward me. "Oh, knock it off!" I tell him.

He makes a high-pitched clicking sound then dives under the surface. Goliath doesn't speak English (or Spanish or French) but his whole demeanor begs, "Play with Me." "I can't play. I have to find Rayna. Have you seen her?" Yes, I really just did ask a whale that. And, no, he doesn't answer.

Instead, half his body launches from the water and lands in a sideways belly flop. The resulting tsunami topples the jet ski.

I am in the water. Fan-flipping-tastic.

Goliath pauses and swims, pauses and swims, waiting for me to regain control over my initial shock and, if he's lucky, my temper. "I told you I couldn't play!"

As I chastise a ginormous whale, I catch the sudden glint of something below us. And I realize too late that it's my car keys shimmering in the last of the dying sunlight as they make their way to the bottom of the Atlantic Ocean. I must have lost them out of my jeans pocket when I flipped over. The keys sink down,

down, freaking down. And suddenly I know what it feels like to be a fish chasing a shiny lure.

I dive after them, and the deeper I go, the better my eyes adjust to the dark. Goliath thinks I'm playing with him after all, but he seems confused about the rules, so he keeps a distance and swims circles around me while I spiral down after the taunting set of keys. His growing wake disturbs the steady fall of them, and they swirl and cut through the water erratically.

I snag them right before they touch bottom, so I shouldn't be as proud as I am when I say, "Ah ha!" It's not like I saved them from any real danger, like a lava pit or something, but there's still a tiny, pathetic sense of accomplishment that washes over me. I grin up at Goliath, triumphant.

That's when the pulse hits me like a physical blow. It saturates the water around me, choking off my chance for escape. It's so strong, so close. Too close. In fact, because of my Half-Breed status, if I can sense *anyone*, they're too close. If a pulse is this strong, they're *way* too close.

The scream, loud and terrified and desperate, comes from the direction of the pulse. I can tell it's a female's scream. A female Syrena.

I already know it's something I can't turn away from. I'm cursed with proximity. Close enough to help, too close to escape with a clean conscience. "Goliath. Take me toward that sound. Hurry."

He swoops down. I grasp his fin. The fact that I'm being chauffeured by a whale is not entirely lost on me, but whoever has been screaming does it again and I decide to be impressed by this phenomenon later. Goliath seems to sense the urgency; we glide through the water faster than I realized he could travel. It helps that each swipe of his fin pushes us about three school buses ahead at a time.

But even at this speed, we're too late. The pulse disappears as quickly as it came. *Is she dead? Please no, please no, please no.* I don't even know this person, but I do recognize the sick feeling swirling in my stomach. It's the same feeling I got when I realized that Chloe had been attacked by a shark. It's the feeling I got when I knew she was dead.

Then I see it. The belly of a boat bobbing in the water ahead of us. A boat. Humans. The relief lasts for only a second. Sharks were not the worse-case scenario after all. Yes, sharks are an immediate threat and dangerous and deadly. But shark attacks only impact the person being attacked. They might maim, they might kill, and it would be sad and horrible. But when it's over, it's over. The shark leaves. Humans, if they capture a Syrena, will keep coming and coming until they harvest every inch of Syrena territory.

A human attack impacts *all* Syrena.

"Let's go up, Goliath. But not all the way. You stay down here." It's silly for me to whisper, but it helps me feel stealthier.

Goliath eases me upward and I quietly break the surface, allowing only my eyes to peek over the waves. I hate what I see.

A young Syrena female, maybe nine or ten years old as far as I can tell, writhes in a net by the side of the boat. Two men. They could be twins with their matching camouflage overalls, sunburned faces, and curly hair escaping in all directions from under their sports caps. Except that one has gray hair and the other has black. Probably father and son.

Dad and Junior are frantically pulling the rope to bring her in, seemingly taken aback by her screams. I'm not sure they realize what they've caught—maybe they mistook her for a human and thought they were saving her. Which could work to her advantage, if she were to calm down and think about it. But she's too panicked to change into human form. Even now, she uses what little water the net soaked up to try to Blend. Her body looks like a puzzle of net and skin and fin and long sopping black hair. It's unsettling to watch.

Especially because it's much too late to hide what she is. Even now, the older fisherman begins to realize their fantastic luck, though the disbelief is still fresh on his face. "A mermaid . . ." It sounds more like a question than a statement. "Look, Don, it's a real live mermaid!"

The one called Don is so dumbfounded that he forgets to hold on to the rope. His new shiny mermaid splashes back into the water entangled in fear and net.

I decide that's the best chance I'm going to get. I duck under and call for Goliath. "Take me to the boat!"

When the girl sees me—another human, in her eyes—she screams again and forgets how close she was to freeing herself from the suffocating grid that is the net. Goliath stops us a few feet under her and I hold up my hands.

"It's okay," I tell her. "I'll help you. I'm . . . I'm Syrena, too." *Oh, Galen is going to kill me.*

My confession is enough to halt her exertions. Her eyes just might pop out of her pretty little face. She readjusts quickly though, tearing her glare from me to concentrate on the task at hand. "No, you're not!" she says, tugging at the rope too erratically to make progress. "You're just tricking me. Tricky humans." But she pauses again, studies the water between us. I'm about to ask if she can sense me like I can sense her.

All at once, the net is jerked back up. Her screams are enveloped by the air above.

I know what I have to do. And Galen won't like it.

But I push that consideration from my mind. Galen isn't here, but if he was, he would help her. I know he would. I don't waste another thought on it. I push through to the surface. "Hey! Let my little sister go!"

This almost stupefies Don into releasing the rope a second time, but good ole Dad catches it and pulls. "Get it together, Don! Do you know how rich we are right now? Pull her in! I'll get the other one."

Nice. The Syrena thinks I'm human and the humans think I'm Syrena. "Let her go or I'm calling the coast guard," I say with more confidence than I feel. After all, this young girl and I look nothing alike. She has the beautiful Syrena coloring, while I probably look like a cadaver floating in the water. But it's worth a shot, right? "And our parents prosecute."

This is enough to season their enthusiasm with a pinch of doubt. It all unfolds in their expressions: *Do mermaids talk? Do they know how to call the coast guard? Do they prosecute offenders? Did that really just happen?*

Don shakes his head as if he's come out of a trance. "Don't listen to her, Paw. That's what mermaids do, remember? They sing fishermen to their death! Haven't you heard the stories? And don't look her in the eye, neither, Paw. They hypnotize you with their eyes."

Well, crap.

But at least *she* heard the exchange, and she suddenly seems to realize I'm not with them after all. "Help me!" she screams, reaching her hands to me through the net as they pull her in. Don pokes her with his finger, the same way one might touch paint to see if it's dry. Paw laughs when she slaps his overgrown son.

But Paw doesn't think it's quite so funny when she bites the meaty part of his own hand, that juicy part where thumb and index connect in a tender knot. "She bit me! The little witch bit me. What's going to happen to me, Don? Will I turn into a mermaid?"

Don sneers. "I swear you old folks are gullible. Everyone knows you don't turn into a mermaid—"

And it's all I can stomach. I dive below, drowning out the sounds of Tweedle Dee and Tweedle Dumbass with a hard underwater doggie paddle to get to my pet whale. "Please, Goliath. You have to flip the boat over. Hurry!"

My heart drops as Goliath swims away from me. Did he not understand what I said? Is he afraid? Could I blame him if he was? Still, with his rapidly vanishing fin goes my only chance for helping this young Syrena—and possibly my only chance for making it back to Galen's house anytime soon.

Just when I feel a sob creeping into my throat, threatening to escape the hopeless depths of me, I see Goliath. And he's heading straight toward me. I shriek and move out of the way. Surely he doesn't mean to head butt me, right? He swooshes past me and up up up. His passing momentum spins me around in a little Emma whirlpool. A loud thud resounds through the water. He's ramming the boat. It topples, but doesn't tip all the way over. I hear the muffled screams of Daddy and Don above. We're definitely on the right track.

"Again, Goliath!"

Again he disappears, this time for a few seconds longer. By now I've wised up enough to give him a wide berth. He zips past me, and I think for sure this time he'll tip it.

He doesn't disappoint. The belly of the boat disappears, flipped on its back like a submissive dog. Fishing poles and cans and boots taper to the bottom of the ocean, followed by one, two, three big splashes. It doesn't take a PhD to know which belong to the humans. Turns out, Paw and Don don't blend in very well in their camouflage overalls.

Still, they swim well enough. I make my way toward the wildly thrashing net. "Calm down," I tell her. "Let me help you." To my relief, she stops fighting.

I take a minute to examine the net that hangs suspended around her like a holey parachute as she descends in slow motion. I pull and twist and tug. All the while, she watches me. Above us, two headless bodies weighed down with droopy overalls tread water and talk between themselves at the surface. They're way too calm.

Don swims under and pokes his head up into the air bubble created by the toppled boat. I don't know what he's looking for but it can't be good. As I disentangle the net piece by piece, I try to pull her deeper and deeper. "I think they're up to something," I tell her. "We need to go deeper, where they can't get us. Humans can't hold their breath very long."

Don emerges from the upturned boat. With a harpoon. He surfaces briefly for air, then he dives toward us. All at once, the young Syrena grabs my wrist through the net and wrenches me down with her, faster than I could have pulled us alone.

Don takes aim. And it's not at us.

"*No!*" But it's all I can get out before the spear embeds into Goliath's side. He makes a horrible sound, a sound that turns my heart into shrapnel. I tug to get free from the little Syrena pulling me away from the men, away from the surface. Away from Goliath.

"I have to go back," I tell her. "The whale. He's my friend. And he's hurt."

She nods and releases me.

"But you keep going," I say. "If you can swim with the net, find others who can help you get loose. Don't come back to the surface. Go!"

I turn from her in time to see Goliath plummet—instincts must be kicking in that deeper is safer. A thin, broken trail of blood chases after him, seeping from where the spear still pierces his flesh. Still, judging by how much of the harpoon still protrudes from his body, I think it's only a shallow wound. I'm instantly relieved, and then instantly disgusted that I'm relieved. *Who cares how shallow the wound is, idiot? He's hurt.*

I open my mouth to call for him, but close it again. It would be stupid—and selfish—for me to distract him from leaving, even if I just wanted to make sure he'll be okay. After all, it's my fault this happened to him in the first place. I want to tell him how sorry I am that this happened. That I got him into this when all he wanted to do was play. And how thankful I am that he helped. I decide that no matter what, I'll find a way to make him understand how horrible I feel. How grateful I am.

I glance back to the surface where the two stupid fishermen struggle with the clasps of their newly donned life jackets. Life jackets that look much too small to keep those woolly mammoths afloat.

Deciding that I've done all the damage and good I can do, I swim deeper and away from the men. Hopefully someone knows where they are, or at least where to look, and will send the coast guard to help them after a while. Hopefully, after an extended while.

In the meantime, I'm hoping I come across a pod of dolphins to hitch a ride with. Otherwise, it's a long swim home.

16

GALEN WATCHES hunters outside the Arena corral fish into a frenzy. Expertly, they throw traditional seaweed nets into the maelstrom of tuna. The nets, which have large rocks tied at each corner, drag the fish to the bottom, keeping them alive until they're ready to be eaten. The waters around the Boundary are ideal for many types of fish to flourish. The reefs and atolls make for a variety of plant life and fish. Even giant clams can be found here—one tasty clam can feed at least twenty Syrena for the day.

But Galen didn't come to the Arena to watch the hunters wrangle up the morning meal for the attendants of the tribunal. He came to find Toraf before today's session starts. He's had little time with his friend amid the recent turn of events, so Galen can only watch his reactions from afar, which doesn't offer much hint.

Galen finds him where he'd expected to, poised just above

the sand at the end of the Arena. Others may not notice it, because an angry Toraf is truly a rare thing to behold, but Galen can practically feel the animosity emanating from his friend. Which is why he casually bumps into him, taking care to be overly apologetic.

"Oh, sorry about that, minnow. I didn't even see you there." Galen mimics Toraf's demeanor, crossing his arms and staring ahead of them. What they're supposed to be staring at, he's not sure.

His effort is rewarded with a slight upward curve of his friend's mouth. "Oh, don't think twice about it, tadpole. I know it must be difficult to swim straight with a whale's tail."

Galen scowls, taking care not to glance down at his fin. Ever since they went to retrieve Grom, he's been sore all below the waist, but he'd just attributed it to tension from finding Nalia, and then the whole tribunal mess—not to mention, hovering in place for hours at a time. Still, he did examine his fin the evening before, hoping to massage out any knots he found, but was a bit shocked to see that his fin span seemed to have widened. He decided that he was letting his imagination get the better of him. Now he's not so sure. "What do you mean?" he says lightly.

Toraf nods down toward the sand. "You know what I mean. Looks like you have the red fever."

"The red fever bloats you all over, idiot. Right before it kills you. It doesn't make your fin grow wider. Besides, the red tide hasn't been bad for years now." But Toraf already knows what the red fever looks like. Not long after he first became a Tracker, Toraf was commissioned to find an older Syrena who had gone off on his own to die after he'd been caught in what the humans call the red tide. Toraf was forced to tie seaweed around the old one's fin and pull his body to the Cave of Memories.

No, he doesn't think I have the red fever.

Toraf allows himself a long look at Galen's fin. If it were anyone else, Galen would consider it rude. "Does it hurt?"

"It's sore."

"Have you asked anyone about it?"

"I've had other things on my mind." Which is the truth. Galen really hadn't given it much thought until right now. Now that it has been noticed by someone else.

Toraf pulls his own fin around and after a few seconds of twisting and bending, he's able to measure it against his torso. It spans from his neck to where his waist turns into velvety tail. He nods to Galen to do the same. Galen is horrified to find that *his* fin now spans from the top of his head to well below his waist. *It really does look like a whale tail.*

"I don't know how I feel about that," Toraf says, thoughtful. "I've gotten used to having the most impressive fin out of the two us."

Galen grins, letting his tail fall. "For a minute there I thought you really cared."

Toraf shrugs. "Being self-conscious doesn't suit you."

Galen follows his gaze back out into the sea ahead of them. "So what do you think about yesterday's tribunal?"

"I think I know where Nalia and Emma get their temper."

Galen laughs. "I thought Jagen was going to pass out when Antonis grabbed him."

"He's not very good at interacting with others anymore, is he?"

"I wonder if he ever was. I told you how crazy Nalia always acted. Could be a family trait."

It looks like Toraf might actually smile but instead his gaze jerks back out to sea, a new scowl on his face.

"Oh, no," Galen groans. "What is it?" *Please don't say Emma. Please don't say Emma.*

"Rayna," Toraf says through clenched teeth. "She's heading straight for us."

That's almost as bad. Of course, it could be worse, considering all that happened yesterday. Jagen's outrageous claims—not to mention King Antonis's wild display of temper—landed all the Royals under Archival restriction. They must now keep within the narrow confines of the Boundary until the tribunal ends. Emma's presence would more than complicate things. Everyone is already suspicious of the Royals; what would the council of Archives think if they knew the Royals were hiding the existence of a Half-Breed? It would ruin any hope they have—what little there may be, that is—of getting a positive verdict back from the council.

No, Rayna's arrival isn't the worst thing that could happen—unless, of course, it means Emma is in some sort of trouble. But Toraf would tell him if Rayna were swimming with more urgency than normal, wouldn't he? Still, Rayna's unannounced visit isn't a good thing. Grom and Toraf will share the same foul mood. Plus there's always the issue of Rayna's mouth. But what did they expect? Rayna has never been especially fond of being left out. He knew it was just a matter of time. "You have to meet her, tell her to turn around before she gets in the Boundary."

Toraf shakes his head. "She's been in range for a while now.

She started this way yesterday while the tribunal was in session. While I couldn't do anything about it." Toraf turns to Galen. "Trackers have already sensed her. She passed within range of at least two Poseidon Trackers on the way. They're following her."

"How long until she's here?" Galen still can't sense her, so she's still a good distance away. "Why can't you just go meet her?"

"We're being watched as we speak." He inclines his head to their left—the general direction in which Galen feels Jagen's pulse. A pulse that gets stronger by the second. *He's coming toward us.*

"Shark," Galen mutters.

Toraf nods. "I know. But before he's close, there's something I need to tell you." He turns to Galen. "Emma was in the water yesterday, too."

Galen pinches the bridge of his nose. "Great."

"She was with someone, Galen. One of us."

"What? Who? Why? Great. That's just great."

Toraf shakes his head almost indiscernibly. "Not so loud. I'm telling you, they've got ten Trackers on you right now." He sighs. "It was Jasa."

"Jasa? I don't know her."

"I do. She's a fingerling, ten seasons old. I overheard her mother, Kana, telling one of the Archives that she's been disappearing, going off on her own. I think . . . I think she talked to Emma. They were very close to each other. Close enough for a long enough time that they could've talked. The weird thing is . . . Emma wasn't in the water at all, and then suddenly she was, like she was on a boat or something and jumped in."

"I swear if—" Galen starts to name all kinds of ways to kill

Rachel if she's involved, but he's cut off by the sound of his new favorite person to loathe approaching.

"Highness, I've heard your lovely sister plans to join us soon," Jagen says from behind them. "What a happy reunion."

Galen rolls his eyes before turning to face him. "You are correct, Jagen. Rayna has missed you. She loves that face you make when you're upset. She says it's the best impression of a rockfish she's ever seen."

Jagen doesn't like this. His lips curl into a snarl. "Go ahead, young prince. Have a laugh at my expense. I assure you it will be the last time."

Toraf glides in front of Galen. "That sounds a lot like a threat. To my knowledge, threatening a Royal is still illegal."

Galen grabs his shoulder. "It's fine, Toraf. Let this squid release his ink. Ink will only last so long before it fades away in the current. When his protective cloud is gone, everyone will see what's really going on here."

Jagen nods. "We shall see, young ones." He rakes his eyes over Toraf. "Tell your mate that she stays with the rest of the Royals. If she tries to leave, I'll have her thrown in the Ice Caverns. She can wait there until the rest of you join her."

Toraf starts toward Jagen again, but Galen holds him back. "This is not the time," Galen says. Jagen gives Toraf a smug smile. Galen adds, "Besides, you saw his face when Antonis had him by the throat. We don't want him to faint before things get interesting, do we?"

To Galen's dismay, Jagen laughs. "Things have already gotten interesting, Highness. See you soon."

~ ~ ~

Galen waits with Toraf until Rayna arrives. She is accompanied by two Poseidon Trackers. When she sees Toraf, she throws herself into his arms. He hugs her, but then pushes her back. "You're in so much trouble, princess," he tells her. It's the first time Galen has ever seen him be truly stern with his sister.

"It looks like *you're* the one in trouble. What's taking so long?"

"The Archives have convened a tribunal," Toraf says. "For the last few days, they've been trying to verify whether or not Emma's mother is really the Poseidon heir."

That's the nice version of the story, Galen thinks to himself. *Wait until she hears everything.*

"What? That's dumb. Tribunals only last a few hours. You've been gone for days. And why did these idiots follow me?" She motions toward the Trackers. They grin as they swim away—to the Loyal section.

Toraf sighs. "Other tribunals are about simple things, like thievery. This one is . . . You shouldn't have come here. I told you not to come, no matter what."

"Emma said I should come," she says.

"That's a lie," Galen says, recognizing the slight flinch in her eye when she's not telling the truth. "And why was Emma in the water?"

Her eyes go round as oysters. "She was? I didn't know. Rachel bought us some jet skeezers. She must have taken one out."

Galen rolls his eyes. "What else? What *else* could go wrong?"

Toraf snorts. "Don't invite trouble, Highness."

"Don't call me Highness."

Just then, Tandel calls the tribunal to order and the Royals are ushered to their place in the Arena.

"*Highness*," Toraf hisses with a smirk as he swims in the direction of the Triton section.

Galen is envious of his friend's inconspicuous viewpoint in the Arena. All the Royals must stay in the center. Galen can't decide if it's for their protection or to assure that they don't escape their own tribunal. Probably both. After all, there are those here still devoted to the Royals.

But Toraf is lucky. He's not a true Royal; since he's only mated to one, he does not have the same restrictions that Galen and his family have. Neither does Paca, who takes her place in the section of Loyals next to her conniving father.

Tandel begins. "My friends, thank you for your patience. Patience, because this is the longest tribunal in the known history of our kind." He smiles. Galen has to admit that Tandel has done his duty, acting neutrally throughout the duration of the trial. If he is secretly a Loyal, Galen can't tell.

"We are hoping that today will show us the end of the debate. To that end, King Antonis would like to address the audience. I turn the stone over to him."

Antonis is met with a disgruntled roar from the Loyal section. He hovers over the stone, his profile casting a wave-distorted shadow in the sand in front of him. "My friends, I must first begin by apologizing. For my actions yesterday, yes. But for so much more. Jagen's accusations upset me very much. They upset me because some of those accusations were true."

This prompts a murmur from the crowd. Antonis continues. "Jagen said that I have neglected my duty as the leader of the Poseidon territory. This is true. Friends, you remember how distraught I was when my mate, Queen Aja, died. But I took comfort in my daughter, the way my Aja would have wanted me to. When I thought I'd lost Nalia, as well . . . It was more than I could bear. Life did not seem worth living, friends. I did not think you deserved a ruler who could not even protect his own family. If the law would have given me a way out of ruling, I would have taken it."

The king pauses, pinching the bridge of his nose. Tandel reaches out to comfort him, but Antonis waves him off. "No. I want to finish. Please." Galen wonders if Tandel and Antonis are old friends.

Antonis looks back up into the audience, searching, scrutinizing each expectant face. "You all know what happened after the explosion. That Nalia was presumed dead. And that I presumed Grom, now the Triton king, had killed her. I am ashamed of the things I accused him of. I was irrational, friends. Driven mad by grief. But that is no excuse for abandoning you, for abandoning my duty as king. I should have taken another mate, produced another heir."

Antonis swims slightly away from the stone, toward the section of Loyals. "But friends, my daughter is not dead." He turns to Nalia, gives her an adoring smile. "She is here, among the Royals, as is her place. She has returned to us. When she fled to land all those seasons ago, she was young and afraid. And she was grief-stricken, having thought she killed her future mate. Take the time, friends, to imagine what that feels like."

The Poseidon king folds his arms behind his back. "I do not make excuses for what she did; fleeing from her kind, living on land was wrong. She broke the law. But so have many of you here today. Jagen has acted treasonously toward the Royals, and has forsaken the law handed down from our great generals. He has accused the Royals of unimaginable things. Many of you have followed his lead. I beg you today to desist in this madness. To accept Nalia as the Poseidon heir. To reunite her with her intended mate, Grom. But more than that. I beg you to reunite the kingdoms of Triton and Poseidon once more. Just as the generals always intended."

The Loyals give a cry of outrage, but for a moment it is drowned out by the applause of slapping tails in the Arena. In fact, some of the Loyals leave their companions and move to the Triton and Poseidon sections.

Jagen is quick to recover. He swims to Tandel and whispers something to the old Archive. Tandel nods, his expression eager to help.

Tandel addresses the Arena over the continuous drone of the crowd. "Friends, I would like to invite Jagen up to speak again. It has come to our attention that he has some new information."

Jagen graciously takes the center stone of the Arena. "Friends, don't be hasty in gifting the Royals with your trust once again. Trust must be *earned*. Don't be enchanted by the words of a king you have not seen in too many seasons." He chides the audience with a disappointed look. "As it turns out, I do indeed have new information."

Jagen smiles viciously at the small section of Royals behind the center stone. "No doubt you've noticed the sudden presence of Princess Rayna. For the past few days, we have been searching for her, without the cooperation of the Royals. We feel it is important to hear her testimony, as her future is determined by the outcome of this tribunal as well."

"*What* is he talking about?" Rayna snarls to Galen.

"I don't know," he whispers. "I didn't know they were looking for you." Which is the truth. And it's also very clever on Jagen's part. *Of course he didn't have the cooperation of the Royals—he never told us he was looking for her.* But that might be for the better, since none of them were likely to give up her location anyway. What's more is that Jagen sees value in Rayna's testimony. Putting her on the center stone and provoking her temper is the best way to turn the rest of the crowd against the Royals. Galen exchanges a concerned look with Grom.

"If it would please you, friends," Jagen continues, "I would like to inquire of her Highness as to her whereabouts, and her involvement in the appearance of the alleged Poseidon heir."

The audience seems to applaud as one, beating their fins against each other. The sound reverberates through the Arena. Jagen smiles. "Without further delay, I invite Princess Rayna to the center stone."

Rayna grabs Galen's hand. "I don't want to go to the center stone."

"I know. Just stay calm. You'll be okay."

She shoots him a look. "You don't believe that."

"I believe it, *if* you keep your temper in check. Toraf is over there in section Triton. Just keep your eyes on him. Don't look at the crowd."

She takes in a breath. "I don't say things the right way."

"I know."

"And he's going to make me mad."

"I know."

"I shouldn't have come back."

I know. Galen places his hand on the small of her back and propels her forward. He wishes she'd come just a little sooner—she could have changed into the traditional Syrena seaweed wrap for females. Now she has to take the center stone wearing the top half of a purple human swimsuit. Jagen can be relied upon to exploit that to his full advantage.

Rayna takes forever to reach the center stone. Jagen rolls his eyes.

Tandel greets Rayna warmly. "Thank you for honoring us with your presence, Highness. Jagen has expressed the desire for your testimony on the issues at hand. Please start with where you have been, princess. Jagen has reported that Trackers have not been able to find you."

Rayna flounders for a moment, then straightens up the moment she finds Toraf in the crowd. It's as if confidence has inflated her; she pokes her chest out and lifts her chin. Galen's not sure if that's good or bad. "I was on land."

"I'm sorry, Highness, but would you mind speaking louder?" Tandel coaxes.

"I can't," she croaks. "My voice has left me."

"How convenient," Jagen sneers.

She crosses her arms at him. Beside Galen, Grom stiffens. There's no telling what she's about to say. But thankfully, Rayna seems to remember Galen's advice to keep her temper. She uncrosses her arms and relaxes. A little. She looks at Tandel. "You can appoint someone to speak for me, if you want. I can't talk, but it doesn't mean I don't have anything to say."

Tandel nods. "Of course, Highness." He motions for a female Archive, Atta, to come to the center. "Atta will assist you, princess. She serves on the council for this tribunal and is therefore a neutral party in these proceedings. Please tell her what you wish our friends in the Arena to know. She will relay your words."

Rayna nods. "Fine. I said I could not be Tracked because I was on land." Atta relays her answer to the Arena.

"And why were you on land, Highness?" Tandel asks.

Rayna mulls over this for a moment. She glances back at Galen in askance. He shrugs. He's not sure how she should respond. The truth would be irretrievably condemning. But what could she possibly say that will make any sense? She turns back to Tandel. "I was on land because I was afraid for my life." She waits for Atta to transfer her comment to the rest of them. Then she continues. "Everyone knows Jagen has been guilty of conspiracy for many seasons. I've known for a while that the Royals would be in danger somehow. Especially when he had Paca pretend to have the Gift of Poseidon."

An irate Jagen swims to the center stone. Rayna halts him. "What do you think you're doing? You can see that it's my turn to give testimony. *You* wanted this, remember?" Atta looks as if she'd rather not repeat that, but Rayna gives her a reproving look. The Archive concedes. The Arena hums with scandal when they hear.

Jagen whirls on the crowd. "Do you hear the nonsense she has spoken? She's calling into question your good judgment! You have already seen, have already decided for yourselves that my own Paca has the Gift of Poseidon. She has demonstrated it for you at your every request. This Royal is calling me, and all of you, liars! How can we trust anything she says? Look at her."

He points to her bathing suit top. "She wasn't hiding from me. She was enjoying herself on land, living like a human. It seems having an ambassador to humans for a brother has been quite convenient for our young princess."

Galen feels his throat constricting. The crowd is wild with agitation.

Rayna lunges for Jagen. "You slithering eel!" But her voice gives out and she sounds like an angry sea lion trying to make words. Jagen moves out of the way. Trackers seize Rayna and pull her back by the arms. She glares at Atta. "You tell them that I don't like humans. You tell them that I was hiding from Jagen!"

Atta shouts over the disgruntled moans of the assembly, but it falls on deaf ears.

Then a voice speaks up, louder than everyone else. Angrier than everyone else. "She's a liar!" The crowd grows silent.

Because the voice belongs to Toraf.

"What is he *doing*?" Grom says, nudging Galen's shoulder with his own.

Galen watches as Toraf makes his way to the center stone and comes face-to-face with Jagen. Then Toraf, his best friend since they were fingerlings, bows to the traitor. Jagen seems as surprised as Galen feels.

"Toraf!" Rayna shrieks. "What—"

"Someone shut her up," Toraf says, motioning to the Trackers who hold his mate. "I'm tired of listening to her lies."

Jagen is still unsure. He narrows his eyes. "What do you mean?"

"All the Royals are lying. They're covering up for themselves. And I won't be a part of it any longer." Toraf makes eye contact with Galen. He doesn't even flinch when he says, "Especially Prince Galen. He's found a Half-Breed. He's been hiding her existence from all of you."

The entire Arena seems to gasp in unison. Toraf clasps Jagen on the shoulder. Galen feels like he's swallowed a blowfish. "If you will forgive me for my part in it, Jagen, I vow to bring the Half-Breed to you. As proof."

"No!" Nalia screams. She springs forward and almost gets her hands around Toraf's neck before Triton Trackers move in front of him. She wrestles them with the sudden power of a predator. "You disgusting traitor! We trusted you. What have you done?"

Toraf rolls his eyes. He tells Jagen, "I cannot tell you how sick I am of that imposter. I can't believe I almost helped them. I saw Paca's Gift with my own eyes. I don't know how I could have doubted your cause."

Sheer delight spreads on Jagen's face. He cocks his head back and laughs a toxic laugh. "You've done the right thing, Toraf. You are not as foolish as I thought."

"No, I was. You give me too much credit, friend. But I can see now how they've tricked me." Toraf turns to the Arena. "Just as they've tricked all of you for so long. They're not worthy to rule. None of them. I will go and get the Half-Breed and prove to you just how untrustworthy they are. All of them know about her. Every last one. I challenge Prince Galen to deny it."

Galen locks eyes with Toraf. *How could he do this to me? How could he do this to Emma?* Now everyone present knows of her existence. She won't be safe anywhere, not with Jagen in control. Especially because Toraf, the best Tracker in Syrena history, has just vowed to find her and bring her here.

Which will be excessively easy, since he knows exactly where she is. She trusts him. Rachel trusts him. It will be so simple for him. *And I have no way of warning her, of getting to her. All I can do is protect her when she gets here.*

Tandel quiets the crowd, one of his primary duties as of late. When he has achieved control, he turns to Galen. "Your Highness, would you like to address these accusations against you?"

Galen swims to the center stone without taking his eyes off Toraf. "If something happens to her because of you," he whispers to his one-time friend, his voice raw with hurt, "your death will be my priority."

Toraf opens his mouth to say something, but Galen cuts him off to address the crowd. There is nothing Toraf can say to him that will make this right. There is nothing Toraf can say to him that will hurt him more. "I have nothing at all to say to these accusations."

Tandel sighs. "Very well, Highness. Thank you."

Galen swims to the Trackers who hold his sister. His sister who now sobs uncontrollably. "Come on, minnow," he says. "He's not worth your tears."

"Yes, he is," she wails. The Trackers release her to her brother. They're distressed with the task of comforting a hysterical female.

Galen squeezes her to him, but won't let her turn around and look at Toraf. "He isn't. In time you'll see that."

"Why would he bring Emma here, Galen? Why would he do this to us?"

Galen swallows the vomit creeping its way into his throat. "I don't know, minnow. I don't know."

Below, his fin throbs with pent-up tension. But it's nothing compared to the sharp ache in his heart. The twins take their place with the rest of the Royals.

Jagen claims the center stone. He can barely contain his glee. "Friends, we were hoping to end our debate today, which has turned out to be the greatest tribunal in the history of our kind. For many seasons, the Royals have produced generation after generation of useless heirs, heirs who have not shown evidence of the Gifts left to us by our great generals. How long has it been since we've seen the Gift of Poseidon from this Royal line? Too many seasons, I think. And how long has it been since we've seen the Gift of Triton? Friends, we cannot even remember what the Gift of Triton is!"

Jagen clasps his hands behind his back. Leaving the center stone, he approaches the section of Loyals, shaking his head. "We have not seen the Gift because the Royals have strayed. Paca is proof that they have strayed at some point. How else could she possess the Gift? Friends, if I truly believed they were pure Royals, I would serve them faithfully, along with the law they've been representing. But Royals with diluted blood are of no use to us. We must find a new way to survive. We must elect a leader who cares about us more than the human world. Someone who is strong enough to lead even as the Gifts disappear from among us."

He turns to Tandel. "I do not ask that we come to a decision today. All I ask is that we let young Toraf retrieve the Half-Breed abomination. Only when we have this final, solid proof of the betrayal of the Royals will we be able to make a united decision."

The masses roar with approval.

Toraf bows to them one last time before leaving the Arena.

17

I PULL into the driveway of my house and cut the engine. I haven't been here in days but it seems like years. I finagle with my key at the front door and all the smells of home smack me in the face.

I set my backpack on the counter and grab a bottled water from the fridge. It feels good to plop down on my own couch in the living room and stare out of my own bay window. Sure, Galen's house has all the luxuries his fortune can buy. But home is full of luxuries money can't buy. Like Grammy's ugly crocheted blanket. Like the faint smell of Mom's perfume.

Like privacy.

It's been three days since Rayna ditched me. I've spent the bulk of those days with Rachel and it has been strangely awkward. She was furious when she found out what I did. I couldn't even lie about it, because Paw and Don had gone on the local news to tell about their incredible mermaid story and the pale blond girl who showed up. So when I finally make it back to land, sopping wet and tired to the bone, Rachel is waiting for me with more attitude than a little woman like her should really possess. Along with the attitude, I sense a trace of guilt—maybe for not thinking things through. Because let's face it, buying us jet skis wasn't the most brilliant of ideas. Sure, I screwed up. But so did she.

When she was satisfied that I couldn't be identified, she loosened up.

Until the coast guard showed up at Galen's door, that is. They'd found my lost jet ski, but they were very sorry to inform her that it was not in running condition. After they left, she'd gone around the house throwing things, yelling how she hates when cops show up at her house and how they seem to show up all the time since Galen took an interest in me, and how she knew better than to register the damn thing with the state. After that fit, I felt weird being around her, mostly because after she apologized, she went way overboard in making it up to me.

Which is insane. After all, I *did* wreck her new jet ski and attracted the "cops" to her house. All of the things she said were true. But she's having none of it. "You're Galen's sweetheart. I shouldn't have yelled at you." She makes me breakfast, lunch, and dinner. She asks how my day went. She asks me what I want from the store. She does my laundry. She offers to give me pedicures. It's too much. At least with Rayna here, she could divide her efforts between the two of us. Now I'm it.

A bolt of lightning strikes close somewhere on the beach. The weather channel has been calling for severe thunderstorms tonight. Looks like I made it right on time to excuse myself from going back to Galen's for the evening. I call Rachel to let her know.

"You want me to come over? I don't mind driving in it."

"No, no," I say a little too quickly. "That's okay. I'll be fine. You have a night to yourself."

"Don't be silly. I've had plenty of nights to myself."

"Right. But, uh, my house isn't as nice as Galen's house. You probably won't be comfortable here."

"Psh. You know I can sleep anywhere."

At this point I don't know if Rachel is purposely dodging my hints, or if she genuinely doesn't get it. "Actually, I'd like to be alone tonight. If that's okay."

Silence. Then, "Why? Anything I should know about?"

"Yeah. There's no place like home."

More silence. The kind of silence that suggests offense. If she is offended though, she keeps it to herself. "Well. Good night then."

"Good night, Rachel."

The power goes out about an hour later. The storm unfurling outside, minus the comforting hum of electricity in the house, plus the scary movie I'd been watching, equals my nerves rioting. We have a generator, but it's in the garage and I wasn't smart enough to keep a flashlight with me on the couch. Even if I was, I don't actually know how to start the generator.

I stand and wrap the blanket around my shoulders, not because I'm cold but because, stupidly, I feel better protected against the unknown with an extra layer. Each time the lightning illuminates the room—which, thankfully, is often—I memorize the next few steps ahead of me before the dark takes over again. Making my way to the kitchen, I wait for the next lightning to flash so I can open the cabinet where Mom stores her heavy-duty flashlight. As I reach for it, the silhouette of a man's shadow flashes like a black stain against the white cabinets.

I turn around and clutch the flashlight to my chest. What do I do? If I turn the flashlight on, the intruder will know exactly where I am. He'll be able to follow the light right to me. But if I keep it off, I might miss my opportunity to see *him*.

I duck down and peer around the counter. Whoever was standing in the living room isn't there anymore. Goose bumps spring up everywhere—he probably already saw me in the kitchen and is on his way to get me. I wait for a bolt of lightning, then another before I have the courage to crawl across the linoleum and into the hallway.

Which I immediately realize is a stupid move. If he were to appear in front or behind me, there's nowhere to go. I back up, hoping I don't bump into anything. Lightning illuminates the short distance back to the kitchen. My only chance is to make it to the garage. I have to be quick, because the door makes a god-awful noise and sometimes it sticks without shutting all the way. As soon as I open it, he'll know where to find me. But it's the only chance I get.

My hand closes around the knob.

His hand closes around my arm.

I turn around screaming, and slam the flashlight into his face, his neck, his shoulder, I'm not sure which. Suddenly my weapon is ripped from my hands. I hear it land a few feet away on the kitchen floor.

A flash of lightning shows that he is very big. Muscular. And he's not wearing a shirt.

"Were you really crawling around on the floor?" Toraf says.

"Ugh!" I shove him back. "Is that your favorite thing to do? Scare me?"

He snickers. His outline moves toward the living room. "If you're so scared you should lock the doors."

I open my mouth and shut it a couple of times. I *had* forgotten to lock the door to the back deck but it doesn't mean he has to go out of his way to scare the snot out of me. I follow him to the living room and slink to the couch. "What are you doing here? Where's Galen?"

Nothing good ever follows silence like this.

"Emma, I need you to come with me to the Boundary. Right now."

The dark hides his expression, but he sounds dead serious. I try to imagine Toraf dead serious and can't. *The Boundary?* Galen had told me about the Boundary before. It's where they hold the Syrena version of a court trial. It's where people who are troublemakers go. "Why? What's wrong?"

"A lot. I'm not sure how he's done it, what he's promised them, but Jagen has turned both the houses against the Royals. There are Trackers and Archives who have sworn that they don't recognize your mother's pulse. And now Jagen has accused the Royals of straying."

"Straying?" I know what that means in human terms, but in Syrena lingo I have no idea.

"Of adultery. Maybe not these Royals, but he says that some Royals down the line *somewhere* had to have strayed because how

· 159 ·

else would Paca have the Gift of Poseidon?" He scoffs. "I can't really believe this is happening. How could they believe a slimy eel like Jagen?"

Lightning hits close and I get a good look at Toraf. He's as stressed out as he sounds. I let him talk, because it seems like he has more to say, and if not, he needs to vent. "The Royals can't even leave the Boundary now because King Antonis—he's your grandfather, did you know that?—tried to choke Jagen when he made up all these stupid accusations."

He's your grandfather. Technically, I did already know that. I already knew the story of Nalia and Grom, and that Antonis, her father and the Poseidon king, accused Grom of murdering her. But that was out of context. That was when these people were strangers. That was before Mom was Nalia. *I have a grandfather. I have a king for a grandfather. A king fish.*

I clear my throat. "So ... This isn't just about my mom's identity. This is Jagen making his move to take over the kingdoms? And ... you think he's getting away with it?"

"Yes. Exactly."

"But I don't understand. What could I do to stop him? I'm just a Half-Breed."

"You can come with me and show them that you have the true Gift of Poseidon. That Nalia is your mother. It will prove her identity, that the Royals aren't lying, and that they haven't strayed."

"Won't it technically prove that they *have* strayed? I mean, you know how babies are born right? That means my mom and my dad—"

"I know how it works. And, uh, I don't want to talk about

it with you. And I'm pretty sure Galen doesn't want me to, either. But I'm hoping Nalia can be forgiven for all of that, since
she thought Grom was dead. But they don't even believe she *is*
Nalia."

I nod, but the action is lost in the dark. Outside, the storm
seems to be losing momentum. "Galen sent you to get me?"

The long silence gives me the answer. "He doesn't know
you're here?" I ask, licking my lips.

"He knows," Toraf says softly. "But he thinks I'm bringing
you back to turn you over to Jagen."

I swallow. "Are you?"

I see his outline jump up from his chair. "No! It's unbelievable how everyone is so quick to accept I'd turn on them. Have
I ever turned on them? Not once! You should have seen Galen's
face when I told Jagen I'd bring you back. If he could get to me,
he would have killed me, I know it. And Rayna..." A small
strangled sound escapes him. "Triton's trident, Emma. You have
to come with me and make this right. They can't go to the Ice
Caverns thinking I betrayed them."

"I promised Galen I wouldn't get in the water. Now you're
asking me to come with you and show all the Syrena I exist?
He'll freaking kill me. Mom will kill me. They're both bent on
keeping me a secret. They think it's dangerous for me. Why
don't you think that?"

I feel Toraf's weight register on the cushion beside me. Just
then, the power kicks back on. The whole house seems to buzz.
Toraf has tears in his eyes. Tears. He takes my hand in his. "I'm
not going to tell you it's not dangerous for you. It is. But if we
don't do something, the Royals will be sentenced to the Ice

Caverns. You'll never see Galen or your mother again. I'll never see Rayna again."

"But you're mated to Rayna. Doesn't that make you a Royal, too?"

"Not a true Royal, that's not how it works. They're only talking about purebloods. Paca will be exempt, too. If they're sentenced to the Caverns, we'll both be free to choose different mates. But I don't want another mate, Emma. I want Rayna. I always have."

Geez, the boy knows how to make my heart all melty. I bite my lip. "It's that serious? Really?"

He nods. "I wouldn't ask you to risk yourself if it weren't. But I don't see any other way out of it. The Royals give testimony, then one of Jagen's Loyals gives testimony. It's one word against the other, and the crowd is leaning toward the Loyals. I can hear what they're whispering. It doesn't help that Paca can prove that she has the Gift of Poseidon. There's no one to refute it. They have more going for them than we do right now."

"Galen told me that Paca uses hand signals to make dolphins do tricks, like they do at the Gulfarium. The Archives don't think there's something wrong with that? That she can't talk to any other fish?"

"I think they're confused. They haven't seen the Gifts in a long time and Jagen is taking advantage of that. He's making them question what they know."

I pull from his grasp and fold my hands in my lap. I can't look at him right now. Not with the pain in his eyes and the emotion in his voice. I've never seen Toraf like this and I don't like it. He's always been a caricature of himself, the class clown. Now he's risking Galen's trust—and friendship—just by being here. And he's asking me to risk it, too. Still, he would never hurt Rayna . . . Unless it was absolutely necessary. "But I *promised* Galen I wouldn't get in the water."

"We both know you already broke that promise, Emma."

I gasp. But really, I'm not shocked. I was wondering if Toraf sensed me that day. And I was wondering if he told Galen. "It wasn't my fault. I was on a jet ski and Goliath knocked me into the water. He was trying to play."

"So you decided to invite Jasa to join you?"

"Who?"

"The Syrena fingerling you were with. I told you. I sense everything."

Jasa. Her name is Jasa. "Is she okay?"

He nods. "Why wouldn't she be?"

"Some fishermen caught her in their net. I helped her get away. She didn't say anything?"

Of all things, Toraf grins. "No, probably because she wasn't supposed to be off by herself. Telling everyone about you would be telling on herself."

"So . . . Galen doesn't know?" I'm not sure why I care. What Toraf is asking me to do is way worse than helping a young Syrena out of a fisherman's net. He's asking me to expose myself to the entire Syrena world. A Syrena world that thinks I'm an abomination deserving of death. Galen is going to be freaking thrilled.

"That's between you and Galen. I think you should definitely tell him." Toraf shrugs. "Eventually, anyway. But will you come with me now? Will you help me?"

It's not lost on me that Toraf didn't actually answer my question, but I can tell he's not going to fess up either way. But telling Galen about my screwup is the least of my worries. We won't even get the *chance* to fight about it if I don't help Toraf.

I mean, if Toraf, the most laid-back person I've ever met, is worried about everyone we both love, then I should be, too. I know Galen wouldn't want me to come, even to save him. But sometimes Galen doesn't get what he wants. I nod. "You want me to come right now? In the storm?"

He smirks. "Only land dwellers worry about storms."

"Oh, yeah. Wait. We're going to the Boundary? Isn't that, like, in the belly button of the Pacific Ocean or something? There's no way I can swim that far." I pat my piddly human legs for emphasis.

"I can carry you."

"How much time do we have? You're not as fast as Galen and the extra weight will slow you down. How long did it take you to get here anyway?"

He scowls. "Two days, and that was really pushing it. You're right, we won't be fast enough. Jagen might start to doubt my word. Do you think Rachel can help us?"

"There's only one way to find out." I pick up my cell phone and dial the 800 number, then leave her a message. "Rachel, it's Emma. Toraf is here and we need your help getting to Hawaii. Tonight. Call me."

"What's Hawaii?" Toraf asks as I hang up.

"It's an island in the Pacific. If we fly there, we can swim the rest of the way to the Boundary."

Toraf looks almost green. The same green Galen turns when he gets on a plane. "Oh, no. I can't fly. No way."

The phone rings. "Rachel?"

"Hiya, cupcake. I see Toraf found you. What's up?"

"We need the next flight out to Hawaii. And, um, we need some Dramamine for Toraf. A lot, because remember Dr. Milligan said they metabolize it faster than humans."

"I'm on it."

You'd think someone as resourceful as Rachel would know whether or not Toraf was the identical twin of a known terrorist. But nooooo. So we wait by our guard in the corridor of the security office of LAX airport while about a dozen people work to verify our identity.

My identity comes back fine and clean and boring.

Toraf's identity doesn't come back for a few hours. Which is not cool, because he's been puking in the trash can next to our bench seats and it's got to be almost full by now. Because of the regional storms in Jersey, we'd had a rough takeoff. Coupled with the reaction Toraf had to the Dramamine—excitability, no less—it was all I could do to coax him out of the tiny bathroom to get him to sit still and not puke while doing so.

His fingerprints could not be matched and his violet eyes were throwing them for a loop, since they physically verified that they aren't contacts. A lady security officer asked us several times in several different ways why our tickets would be one-way to Hawaii if we lived in Jersey and only had a carry-on bag full of miscellaneous crap that you don't really need. Where were we going? What were we doing?

I'd told them we were going to Honolulu to pick a place to get married and weren't in a hurry to come back, so we only purchased one-way tickets and blah blah blah. It's a BS story and they know it, but sometimes BS stories can't be proven false. Finally, I asked for an attorney, and since they hadn't charged us with anything, and *couldn't* charge us with anything, they decided to let us go. For crying out loud.

I can't decide if I'm relieved or nervous that Toraf's seat is a couple of rows back on our flight to Honolulu. On the plus side, I don't have to be bothered every time he goes to the bathroom to upchuck. Then again, I can't keep my eye on him, either, in case he doesn't know how to act or respond to nosy strangers who can't mind their own business. I peek around my seat and roll my eyes.

He's seated next to two girls, about my age and obviously traveling together, and they're trying nonstop to start a conversation with him. Poor, poor Toraf. It must be a hard-knock life to have inherited the exquisite Syrena features. It's all he can do not to puke in their laps. A small part of me wishes that he would, so they'd shut up and leave him alone and I could maybe close my eyes for two seconds. From here I can hear him squirm in his seat, which is about four times too small for a built Syrena male. His shoulder and biceps protrude into the aisle, so he's constantly getting bumped. Oy.

Truthfully though, playing mother to Toraf has helped keep my mind off the potential things to come. Until now. The possibility that I'll be killed keeps coming to mind. Or even worse, Galen might not ever speak to me again. That would be worse than death, I think.

Not to mention all this school I've missed. It's four in the morning on a Wednesday and I'm leaving California, headed to Hawaii, then to who-knows-where and will return who-knows-when. I'm going to have to come up with a fantastic excuse to give my guidance counselor for all of these absences, especially if I'm still interested in all the scholarships I filled out applications for. I should have had Rachel write a note or something before we left. But knowing Rachel, she might have already thought of that.

In fact, knowing Rachel, she can probably make the absences disappear.

Am I really thinking about school when my mom and Galen are in trouble? Yes, yes I am. Because this is the life bequeathed to me. Part human, part fish. Part straight-A student, part possessor of the Gift of Poseidon. Yep, I'm a natural-born overachiever.

Fan-flipping-tastic.

Behind me, I hear the most obnoxious belch in history. "Excuse me," Toraf says. I hear him wrestle with his buckle and make a hasty retreat to the bathroom. And I'm officially glad I'm not sitting next to him. Let's face it. He's a loud puker.

Syrena were not meant to fly.

When we land, Toraf is asleep. He doesn't even wake up despite the wobbly landing and the giggling girls and the announcement of "Aloha" by the captain. When everyone has disembarked I make my way back to Toraf and shake him until he wakes up. His breath smells like slightly microwaved death.

"We're in Hawaii," I tell him. "Time to swim."

We take a cab to a hotel on the beach. We check in under the reservations Rachel made for us and dump our luggage in the room. I decide that if I ever get to come back here under different, nonstressful circumstances, I will stay at this hotel and drink fruity drinks and lay in the sand until my skin looks like it had a makeout session with the sun. But today, I'm looking for an inconspicuous way into the water.

We head out of the lobby and get waylaid by hula dancers in grass skirts handing out necklaces of flowers. Apparently Toraf doesn't like necklaces of flowers; as one of the women raises it above his head, he slaps her hand away. I show him, as I accept the gift around my neck, that the woman with the coconut boobs was just trying to be his friend. Just like all the women he's come across so far.

"Humans are too weird," he whispers, unconvinced. I wonder what Toraf would think of Disney World.

Our hotel is right on the water, so we pass through the lobby to the back. The beach is lined with lounge chairs and umbrellas and people scantily clad and people who shouldn't be scantily clad. The smell of coconut and sunscreen linger on the breeze that wafts through the abundant palm trees. It's a paradise I can't enjoy.

We walk the beach looking for private charter but they've all been rented well in advance. I'm flirting with the idea of renting a jet ski to take us farther out faster than Toraf could, but I'm bothered by the idea that when we ditch in the Pacific, it would be tantamount to stealing.

And then I see it. Azure Helicopter Tours.

I drag Toraf to the landing pad. "What is that?" he asks suspiciously.

"Um. It's a helicopter."

"What does it do? Triton's trident, it doesn't fly does it? Emma? Emma wait!"

He catches up to me and burps right in my ear. "Stop being a jerkface," I tell him.

"Whatever that is. You don't care about me at all, do you?"

"*You* came for *me*, remember? This is me helping you. Now be quiet while I buy tickets." It's a private ride, no other passengers to worry about. Plus, we're not stealing anything. The helicopter can return to land with its pilot as soon as we're done with our part of the mission.

"Why do we need to fly? The water is *right there*." He points to it longingly. I almost feel bad for him. Almost. But I don't have time for pity.

"Because I think these helicopters can still cover more distance faster than you can haul me. I'm trying to make up for all the time we spent at security in LAX."

"Humans are so *weird*," he mutters again as I walk away. "You do everything backward."

Since this is a sightseeing flight, the pilot, Dan, a thick Hawaiian man with an even thicker accent, takes his time pointing out all the usual tourist stuff, like the fishing industry, the history of the coast, and other things I have no interest in at the moment. The view of the blue water and visible reefs, the chain of islands, and the rich culture would be breathtaking if I weren't preoccupied with crashing a Syrena get-together. I can imagine spending time with Galen here. Exploring the reefs like no human could, playing with the tropical fish, and making Galen wear a lei. But I need to stay focused if I ever want a chance to do it.

When we've flown around for about twenty minutes, I recognize that Dan is taking us back to the landing pad.

"Where are we going?" I ask through the noise-canceling headset. It's difficult to believe I can hardly hear the *whop-whop-whop* of the chopper blades.

Dan's response comes through as clear as the water below us. "Back. The tour is thirty minutes. Would you like to upgrade to the forty-five-minute tour?"

"Not exactly." I've only ever seen this done in the movies and I pray that Rachel's right and money really does buy anything. I pull a hundred dollar bill out of my pocket and show it to him. "Instead of going around the islands, can you take us out that way? I want to see the ocean."

Dan frowns, eyeing the bill. "I'm sorry, but we're not supposed to go anywhere but the designated tour areas."

I pull out two more bills. "I know. But I'm hoping you'll make an exception?"

What Dan doesn't know is that I could do this all day. Rachel gave me enough cash to buy a new car. I'm hoping that she is right, and that everyone—that Dan—has a price.

He scratches his chin. I can tell he's tempted. "We're really not supposed to. I could get fired."

I hand him a wad of hundreds. I have no idea how much is there, but I've got more in the other pocket. "But, Dan, I've been waiting all my life for this helicopter ride. I've been looking forward to it since I was a little kid. If you don't take us out, my heart will be broken. Besides, even if you *did* get fired—which I'm sure you won't because you're just making my dreams come true, right?—I'm betting this would pay the bills for a while." I have no idea what Dan's bills are, if he has a wife and kids, or if whatever. But from his expression, I've hit the nail on the head.

He tests the weight of the bills in his hands. Finally, he sighs. "Fine."

I nearly squeal, and maybe I should because it would add special effects to my story. I grin triumphantly at Toraf, whose complexion has turned a lovely puce shade, just like Galen's did on our way to Destin. My small, expensive victory is lost on him.

Dan takes us out far enough that I can't see the island anymore. He doesn't try to be the ever efficient tourist guide now; apparently we're responsible for our own entertainment way out here. He keeps glancing at the panel in front of him. "This is as far as we go," he announces after a while. "Or we won't have enough fuel to get back."

"Do you think we've gone far enough?" I ask Toraf.

He shakes his head.

"We'll have to swim the rest of the way," I decide as I say it. Dan laughs like I've made a joke.

Toraf nods. "Great. Just get me out of this thing." Then he belches like a drunk.

I look at Dan and point down. "Before we turn back, can we just go lower? I want to see the water close up."

"Oh, sure, sure," he says, and we feel the sensation of gravity kicking in as he descends.

My breath catches as the chopper lowers. Dozens, no wait, *hundreds* of dark shadows skim the surface. I yank on Toraf's sleeve and nod toward the water.

Eyes wide, he taps Dan's shoulder. "We need to go a little farther out, please."

"No can do. I told you, we need all of our fuel to get back."

Slowly, I unstrap the belt. "Just a little lower please? I think I see some fish down there."

"No prob."

I've never skydived, bungee-jumped, or parasailed. As I remove the headset, I try to calculate the fall and can't. Maybe my brain is protecting me from myself and what I'm about to do. I'm not sure of the exact numbers, but I've heard hitting the water from such-and-such height feels like hitting concrete at such-and-such miles per hour. In other words, it's a bone-shattering experience. I seriously doubt those calculations are based on the Syrena bone structure though. In fact, I'm counting on it.

"No lower, okay?" Dan says, looking out his window to the water below. "Oh, you see sharks! Wow, it looks like a feeding frenzy down there. Hey, don't touch that!"

I grip the handle harder, but the door won't budge. Leaning back, I get in the mule-kick position.

"Emma, don't!" Toraf yells. "Those are *sharks*, Emma!"

I take a deep breath. "Wait until I have them under control before you jump." A joint effort from two half-Syrena legs sends the door flying to a watery grave.

"They want proof?" I grumble to myself as I lean into the wind, "I'll show them proof." Right before I hit the water, I can still hear Toraf screaming.

18

IF HIS own future weren't dependent on the outcome of this tribunal, and if Emma weren't entangled in it all now, Galen would find it highly entertaining.

While they wait for Toraf's return with the alleged Half-Breed, the audience has been subjected to a match of conflicting testimonies. The Archive Odon insists that when a Syrena is on land for long periods of time, his or her eyes would fade to blue. He references the wall painting in the Cave of Memories for proof—the same painting that led Galen to conclude that Emma's father was a Half-Breed. Galen remembers the Syrena with the blue eyes on the wall, and how Romul dismissed it as faded paint.

Which is exactly what another Archive, Geta, contends. She chastises Odon for spreading what he very well knows to be a mere myth parents tell their fingerlings to keep them away from land.

Then a Tracker by the name of Freya takes the center stone. She gives testimony that the stranger *is* Nalia—and she would know, since Nalia was her best friend since they were very young. Another Tracker, Fader, offers a completely different judgment. He claims he's known the Poseidon Royals since before Nalia was born, and that sadly she is *not* the Poseidon heir. "I was the first Tracker to memorize her pulse," he says somberly. "And this is not the pulse I kept close to my mind and heart."

Galen can't help but roll his eyes. He's been trying to sort all this out, why so many would tell blatant lies about Nalia's identity. What could Jagen have offered them? The Syrena do not lend themselves to greed and riches like humans do. But, what Galen has come to recognize, thanks to the human history class he takes at Middlepoint High School, is that like humans, Syrena just might crave change—whether the change is good or bad. He's seen a pattern arise from the history of the humans, where humans get disgruntled and dissatisfied with what they have, and they long for change. They even have a proverb warning against it—the grass isn't always greener on the other side. But most of the time, if humans have it in their mind that the grass is greener, there's little anyone can do to change their mind.

Galen feels he's witnessing this human trait firsthand in his Syrena brethren. And that *is* something the Royals are responsible for. When King Antonis divided the kingdoms so long ago, he left room for exactly this. Why *wouldn't* the Syrena crave better leadership? Why *would* they trust the Royals after so many years of allowing this silent feud to persist? What *have* the Royals really done to benefit their followers?

Maybe both houses *should* be left to their own endeavors

under Jagen's guidance. Maybe they can make things better, more peaceful. Some human governments managed to do it, managed to pull together after an overthrow and make something great from the remnants of failure.

But if that happens, what does that mean for the Royals? A lifetime in the Ice Caverns. And a death sentence for Emma. Something he cannot allow.

It doesn't matter what is right and what is wrong anymore. It doesn't matter that Jagen has a valid point, despite his convoluted way of getting to it. It doesn't matter what happens to the kingdoms, what verdict is reached at the end of this torturous tribunal. All that matters is keeping the ones he loves safe.

And I'll do whatever it takes to make that happen.

Galen is startled to find that Grom has taken the center stone. The entire Arena is silent, as if they sense a predator coming. Grom lets them scrutinize him, lets them take in his confident poise, his lifted chin, his squared shoulders. Grom has not been defeated.

His brother begins, "I'm thankful for the opportunity to present my testimony before you today. There is much to consider, and I hope you are all taking all the evidence to heart. We have heard much conflicting testimony in the past few days. We've heard from some Trackers that the stranger is none other than the Poseidon heir. We've heard from others that the stranger could not possibly be the Poseidon heir. What we haven't heard though, is this: if she is not the Poseidon heir, then who is she, friends? How can a stranger even exist among us? And if strangers do exist, how many are there? Where can we find them? How did they come to be strangers to us? These are questions we need answers to, friends, if you decide to believe that she is not Nalia the Poseidon princess.

"You well know my feelings regarding this matter. You know I believe with every part of me that this is Nalia." He turns to her then, and smiles. "The Nalia I loved and lost so many seasons ago. I have never done anything dishonorable to you. Even when I thought all was lost, I sacrificed myself to take a Common as a mate, taking a chance that Paca possesses the Gift of Poseidon and that somehow we have misinterpreted the laws passed down from our generals. I took a chance that somehow the Royals may be useful to you yet. I did not neglect my duty to you, as it has been represented here. But before I speak further, I would ask Paca to present her Gift once more, for your benefit. I want you to see why I chose to make this decision."

Paca swims forward to the center stone. The same shock and confusion she wears on her face thunders through the crowd. *What is he doing?* Even Nalia seems perturbed at his request. Galen cannot see how any good can come of this.

Grom holds his hand up. "My queen, Paca, will you please demonstrate your special Gift to us once more?"

She nods, uncertain and nervous, but says, "Of course, Majesty." Then she waves her hand above her, twisting it. Galen has seen the signal a hundred times at the Gulfarium while visiting Dr. Milligan. "Come to me, pets," she says. "Come."

Galen has also seen enough of Paca to know that she keeps her dolphins close at hand, in case she's asked for a show. They practically follow her everywhere and why shouldn't they? She keeps them full on dead fish, leaving an obvious trail of them behind her wherever she goes. Even now, the dolphins instantly spring from between some Syrena in the Loyal section. Could Grom have arranged for her to have them in the Arena for his testimony?

"Ah, there you are, my pets," she says, nuzzling her nose to one of the three affectionately. "Shall we show our friends what we can do?" She twirls her finger around and around. Of course, the dolphins swim in circles in front of her. The Arena cheers.

Galen catches a glimpse of Rayna rolling her eyes. Grom nods to the crowd as Paca has her "pets" do more fancy tricks. What Grom could be hoping to accomplish by putting her apparent Gift on display, Galen doesn't know. But he wishes he'd get on with it.

After a while, Grom asks Paca to rein in her flippered friends. He smiles at her. "Wonderful, Queen Paca." He turns to Section Loyal. "Would you not agree with me, friends, that she put on a splendid example of the Gift of Poseidon?"

At this the Arena explodes into tail slapping and applause. Grom lets them sound off for a while, then signals for silence again. He turns back to Paca. "My queen, now if you will demonstrate the Gift on some of the other fish around the Arena. Choose any one you'd like." He motions around him, as if the Arena were stocked with a variety just for her.

Paca's eyes flit back and forth between several schools of colorful fish. Some swim close to the surface, some swim undisturbed toward Section Triton. Some swim so close to her that she moves out of their path. She scowls. "The Gift does not work that way, Majesty. It only works with dolphins."

Grom turns to Section Triton. "That is troubling, don't you think, friends? The Gift of Poseidon is meant to feed us, is that not correct? But we do not even eat dolphins. Not only do they taste horrible, but there are not enough dolphins in either territory for us to survive for very long. They do not reproduce fast enough for any lasting food source. Friends, dolphins are more companions to us than anything else. Many of you even hunt alongside dolphins, and have done so for many generations. Why would the generals provide a Gift that would only allow us to communicate with, in order to consume, such a scarce but valuable resource to our kind? They wouldn't, friends. They haven't."

Jagen swims to the center to interject, but Grom holds up his hand. "You have already given your testimony, Jagen, several times if I recall. I did not interrupt you once. Not while you insulted my family, my ancestors, or myself. I will not be interrupted now."

Tandel swims between them. "Yes, Jagen, we will return the respect King Grom has shown to us. Please resume your place in the Arena."

Galen exchanges a surprised look with Nalia. Thus far, Tandel has mostly allowed Jagen to interrupt if and when he's pleased. Or rather, he's been unable to stop him, and most who've taken the center stone have backed down from Jagen's aggression. But not Grom.

It's like Tandel is feeding off his brother's confidence and strength.

"You are so quick to accuse the Royals of hiding on land, Jagen. But I will remind you that when Toraf, the best Tracker in the history of our kind, found your Paca, she'd been hiding on land as well. She openly confesses that she did so, in fear that King Antonis would send someone after her because of her Gift. I do not see Paca standing in a tribunal for hiding on land. Why is that?"

By now, the audience has packed in together, as many as will fit, and they seem to lean forward as one, listening to Grom's speech. He turns to Paca. "Do you now deny that you hid on land, Queen Paca? In fear for your life?"

Quietly, she shakes her head.

Grom nods. "Friends, my younger brother, Prince Galen, is the ambassador to the humans, which requires his presence on land from time to time. It is his belief that Paca possesses, not the Gift of Poseidon, but the skills of a human. Prince Galen has informed me that humans use their hands to instruct dolphins. They do this for entertainment. And indeed, it is very entertaining, is it not? But the Gift of Poseidon is not intended for entertainment. It is intended for our very survival. I fail to see how asking dolphins to twirl in place will ensure our survival. What's more, friends, is that it is a well-known fact that the Gift of Poseidon is the result of vocal commands. I have seen with my own eyes, just as you have, that Paca indeed talks to these dolphins. Now I would ask my queen to instruct them to action without using her hands."

Paca bites her lip. "My pets are tired, Highness. They can sense the tension among us and it makes them nervous."

"Of course, I understand that, my queen," Grom says, not unkindly. "But I must insist that you do it, just the same."

She looks to her father for help, but Jagen does nothing except seethe in his rapidly declining section of Loyals. Galen swells with pride for his brother.

That is, until he senses Emma. Toraf is close behind her.

No!

Now is the worst possible time for Toraf to throw a Half-Breed into the now-receding turmoil. To throw *Emma* into it. Grom is doing so well in reasoning with the Arena, winning them back over to the side of logic. Emma's appearance will surely deflate Grom's arguments. Which is probably Toraf's plan.

Rayna tenses up, alert to her mate's presence drawing closer. A Loyal Tracker whispers something in Jagen's ear and he smiles wide. No doubt the Tracker has confirmed Toraf's—and Emma's—imminent arrival.

Grom continues, oblivious to the chaos about to unfold. "It is my belief that the Royals, from this generation and the generations before, have never strayed. It is my belief—" Grom stops, staring past the rim of the Arena over the hot ridges. He glances back to Nalia, who's expression is a mixture of terror and desperation. She nods to him.

Emma.

Suddenly, a commotion begins at the side of the Arena, where Emma's pulse is coming from. *Why is Toraf so far behind her?* The least he could do is see her safely arrived.

Apprehension stabs Galen all over like the sting of a man-o'-war. He silently curses Toraf for bringing her, and Emma for believing whatever it is that he'd told her to convince her to come. He squints in the direction of her pulse and sees what looks like an underwater cloud moving toward the Arena. Galen has never seen anything like it.

And apparently, neither has anyone else.

What could it possibly be? A human military experiment? Are Emma and

Toraf caught in the middle of it? Galen knows that in the past, humans have experimented with their sonar weapons and underwater bombs. Could this be a new way to wage war?

As it moves closer, Galen can make out smaller bodies within the mass. Whales. Sharks. Sea turtles. Stingrays. And he knows exactly what's happening.

The darkening horizon engages the full attention of the Arena; the murmurs grow louder the closer it gets. The darkness approaches like a mist, eclipsing the natural sunlight from the surface.

An eclipse of fish.

With each of his rapid heartbeats, Galen thinks he can feel the actual years disappear from his life span. A wall of every predator imaginable, and every kind of prey swimming in between, fold themselves around the edges of the hot ridges. The food chain hovers toward, over them, around them as a unified force.

And Emma is leading it.

Nalia gasps, and Galen guesses she recognizes the white dot in the middle of the wall. Syrena on the outskirts of the Arena frantically rush to the center, the tribunal all but forgotten in favor of self-preservation. The legion of sea life circles the stadium, effectively barricading the exits and any chance of escaping.

Galen can't decide if he's proud or angry when Emma leaves the safety of her troops to enter the Arena, hitching a ride on the fin of a killer whale. When she's but three fin-lengths away from Galen, she dismisses her escort. "Go back with the others," she tells it. "I'll be fine."

Galen decides on proud. Oh, and completely besotted. She gives him a curt nod to which he grins. Turning to the crowd of ogling Syrena, she says, "I am Emma, daughter of Nalia, true princess of Poseidon."

He hears murmurs of "Half-Breed" but it sounds more like awe than hatred or disgust. And why shouldn't it? They've seen Paca's display of the Gift. Emma's has just put it to shame.

She gives the Arena time to digest that, striking a regal pose she only could have learned from Rayna. An undertone of shock rumbles through the assembly. Some can't take their eyes off the mass of darkness surrounding them. Most can't take their eyes off Emma.

After a while, she raises a finger to her lips, the human signal for silence. The Arena seems to know what she means. "I've come to testify on behalf of the Royals. As you can see, I have some evidence that might have been overlooked." She motions to outside of the Arena, where her collection of meat-eaters hover in wait of her next order.

When Jagen detaches from the crowd and comes toward Emma, Galen puts himself between them. "You're not welcome here, Half-Breed!" he snarls.

Grom joins the three of them at the center stone. A crowd gathers around them. "You yourself summoned her here," Grom says. "Did you not, before everyone, insist that Toraf bring the Half-Breed here?"

"You're Jagen," Emma says, crossing her arms. "You're the cause of all this stupidity. Where is Paca?"

"Paca has nothing to say to a disgusting Half-Breed," Jagen spits. "In fact, none of us here have anything to say to one!" He looks around the growing ring of onlookers. He gets very little support.

Emma treads back, nodding. Searching the faces of the throng surrounding them, she says, "It's true. I am a Half-Breed. Nalia is my mother. My father, a human, is dead. And as for me being welcome here, that's not a decision for one Syrena, but for all of them."

Indecisiveness ripples through the masses. They pack closer to get a better look at Emma. Galen doesn't like the suffocating number of them. Some are still loyal to Jagen. Some of them might want to hurt her.

Jagen pushes against them in warning, forcing them to maintain at least a small center stage. He turns on Emma. "Actually, it *was* decided for them all. Our great generals effected that hundreds of seasons ago. 'No contact with humans.' If you're claiming Syrena heritage, you should at least learn some of our laws, young human."

Emma laughs. Galen recognizes it as her go-to when she's about to prove him wrong about something. But he doesn't want her to prove Jagen wrong. He wants to get her out of here. His whole being thrums with the need to steal her away.

But Emma is determined. "*Now* you're concerned with the laws? I didn't realize you could pick and choose which ones to follow, Jagen. That sounds pretty convenient, huh?" She earns a few nods of approval from their audience, not the least of which comes from King Antonis. He watches her intensely, pride stuck on his face like squid ink. Galen knows the feeling.

Emma pauses, and her whole demeanor changes from huntress to mother as she looks to the accumulation of fish above her. "Those who need air may surface. Come back when you're done. Young ones go first."

Emma turns her attention back to the Syrena. "I possess the Gift of Poseidon. Look around you and deny it."

Jagen's nostrils flare. "Do not let yourselves be charmed by this Half-Breed, as Poseidon did so long ago. That's why Triton ordered all Half-Breeds killed in the first place, is it not? And now you would allow her to defile the sanctity of our Arena with her lies of having the sacred Gift of Poseidon?"

Rayna pushes through the audience, and to Galen's dismay she's holding Toraf's hand. She propels them both into the center. Toraf and Galen exchange nods, but Galen feels as though icicles run through his veins. Emma shouldn't be here. And she's here because of *him*.

"I, for one, do not believe she has the Gift of Poseidon," Rayna says gleefully. "If you have the Gift of Poseidon, make those hammerheads attack Jagen where he stands."

Galen pinches the bridge of his nose. Toraf smirks at him, but Galen will not return the sentiment. Not now and not in a thousand years.

Emma mulls over this for a moment, then points to a female Syrena on the front line of the ring. Galen recognizes her as Tira, a Triton Tracker's daughter. "Pick," Emma tells her.

Tira's lip trembles. She tries to back out of sight, but someone pushes her forward. "Pick . . . Pick what?"

Emma motions to the halo of predators above them, around them, everywhere. "Pick two. Any two you want, and I will have them divide Jagen's body evenly."

"No!" Jagen screams, his face contorted in terror.

Emma cocks her head at him. "Jagen, make up your mind. Didn't you just say you don't believe I have the Gift? So then why should you care if she points to some harmless sharks?"

He clamps his mouth shut, but the look of panic stays.

Tira says, "I couldn't do that, Highness."

Highness! Someone called Emma "Highness"! It's one of the many names she calls Galen when she's mad at him. The irony is not lost on Emma. Her death glare cuts off his snickers.

She turns back to Tira. "Of course you can. There's nothing to worry about because *Paca* has the Gift, remember? Isn't that what you all believe? She would never let any harm come to her own father, would she? I know I wouldn't. So go ahead and pick. Paca will save Jagen."

Clever little angelfish. Galen smirks at Jagen, who won't meet his eyes. Nalia and Grom make their way to the edge of the center. Grom grins at Emma likes she's his own daughter. Which is very weird for Galen.

Tira takes a deep breath. "Okay. Since you put it that way." She eyes the living wall surrounding the Arena and points. "Those two right there. The two striped sharks."

Emma smiles. "Excellent choice." She waves to the tiger sharks. As she opens her mouth to give the command, Galen sees a movement from the corner of his eye. A Loyal Tracker raising his hunting spear.

"Galen, watch out," Rayna rasps, remnants of her voice coming through in fractured rifts of clarity. The water around them seems to rumble. *Could one of the volcanoes be awakening?* An eruption on the full assembly would be the worst possible thing Galen can imagine.

Apparently startled, Emma moves in front of Galen, poised to shield him—from the spear or the eruption, Galen's not sure. In a swift motion, he tucks her back behind him.

The weapon leaves the Tracker's hand. It's the longest second of Galen's life, waiting on that spear. Instinctively, he snatches Emma closer to him, covering every inch of her with him. He feels the small wake of the spear as it swipes past them. That was too close.

At first, Rayna's growl barely gets Galen's attention. After all, it sounds like mere frustration, the familiar beginning of a normal tantrum. But this growl builds, swelling into a roar. The cracks in her voice seem to meld together again, creating something new. Something that hasn't been seen in many, many generations.

She draws up, as if collecting some invisible power around her.

And her scream moves the water.

19

ONE SECOND I'm clinging to Galen for dear life, the next I'm separated from him and pushed back by . . . *Rayna's scream?* Is that possible? I look around at the new faces of Syrena surrounding me, eyeing me as if I pulled them back with me. They are all as shocked as I am. Five seconds ago, we were about thirty yards closer to her.

She blew us over like empty aluminum cans in the wind.

And it looks like she's about to do it again. She turns, takes a big breath of water into her lungs, and screams at a large Syrena male who just tried to spear us, near-hysteria on his face. The momentum of her voice is visible, causing the water in front of her to warp and surge and spread like giant hands reaching toward the Syrena with the weapon.

He doesn't have a chance to get away. The sound wave slaps him dead-on, carries him up and over the crest of the small valley—are those freaking volcanoes?—and through my wall of sea creatures surrounding us. It even pushes back some of the biggest whales.

The upchurned earth starts to settle around us. It looks like a dust storm in the desert, but the water eases the sand back down instead of all at once. The valley looks freshly swept. All eyes are on Rayna, who is now bordering what looks like a major case of hyperventilation.

"Nobody hurts her, you understand?" she says, her voice now completely intact. "I won't . . . I won't let you."

Some of them back away from me. Others talk among themselves. "Gift of Triton," they whisper to one another. Toraf looks like his jaw might fall off.

Rayna has the Gift of Triton. She's living proof that the Royals never strayed. And now I've blown my cover for nothing.

But there is someone who's already recovered, someone who has already thought this through and found the result lacking to his satisfaction. And while everyone—including me—is paying attention to Rayna, he sneaks up behind me out of nowhere. Jagen's pulse hits me just before the sharp jab in my back. I know I've been stabbed, but at first it just feels like a pinch. And then the pain consumes me.

"Die, you filthy Half-Breed!" he growls.

And then I do not sense him anymore. In fact, I don't sense anyone anymore. Not my mother, not Rayna, not Toraf, not Grom.

Not Galen.

Where there used to be a gigantic valley of Syrena pulses hitting me from every direction, there is nothing. The world goes black around me and I can't tell if my eyes are shut or they just stopped seeing. If I'm losing my sensing abilities, if I can't see anything, does that mean I'm dying?

I'm not as brave about it as I hoped I would be. It's one thing to contemplate the possibility of dying. It's another thing to actually be dying. I'm not brave at all. *Ohmysweetgoodness*, I'm scared.

I don't want to die.

And all at once, his pulse resuscitates me, brings me back from the ledge. *Galen.* His arms envelop me and we are speeding, speeding, speeding through the water. I can't even open my eyes—it's like gravity is forcing them shut. I want to sob into his chest but I don't have the strength. I try to speak, but our pace snatches the words from my mouth.

We have never gone this fast. Not ever.

The pain in my back is numbed by the water rushing against it, and I hope it's not tearing the flesh open, and at the same time I hope the salt water is somehow healing it. I know I'm bleeding. I feel warmth gather where the numbness starts. I felt Jagen's weapon pierce me. I felt it touch bone.

I press my face into Galen's neck. He stops immediately, cradles my cheeks in his hands. If we were going by expressions alone, I'd say he was in more pain than me. "Angelfish," he chokes out. "I'm so sorry this happened. We're almost to land. No one can hurt you now. Stay with me, Emma. Oh, please stay with me."

He kisses me all over my face and all I know is that everything up until this point was worth it. The hassle of getting Toraf through security. The terrifying jump from the helicopter. Even the argument I know Galen and I will have about all this later. The agony in my back. The terrifying moment I thought I would die.

He cradles me in his arms princess-style, then picks up the pace again. For a second, it looks like Galen's fin has more than doubled in size. That's when I know I'm hallucinating. I don't know if it's the pain or the loss of blood or both, but I lose consciousness.

Right away, I recognize the scent of Galen's house, of the lemon-scented air fresheners Rachel places strategically throughout. Of the clean linen scent of freshly washed sheets. Of the aroma of fish baking in the oven.

The light of morning creeps into Galen's bedroom window, casting the start of a new day on the white furniture and cool blue-painted walls. I feel him beside me, hear the even sound of his breathing, smell the delicious saltiness of his skin.

I have missed him.

I move to face him, and that's when the pain reminds me that I've recently been stabbed. I bury my face in the pillow, but it doesn't quite muffle my yelp.

"Emma?" Galen says groggily. I feel his hand in my hair, stroking the length of it. "Don't move, angelfish. Stay on your stomach. I'll go tell Rachel you're ready for more pain medicine."

Immediately I disobey and turn my face up to him. He shakes his head. "I've recently learned where your stubbornness comes from."

I grimace/smile. "My mom?"

"Worse. King Antonis. The resemblance is uncanny." He leans down and presses his lips to mine and all too quickly springs back up. "Now, be a good little deviant and stay put while I go get more pain meds."

"Galen," I say.

"Hmmm?"

"How bad am I hurt?"

He caresses the outline of my cheek. His touch could disintegrate me. "Hurt at *all* is bad enough for me."

"Yeah, but you've always been a baby about this stuff." I grin at his faux offense.

"Your mother says it's only a flesh wound. She's been treating it."

"Mom is here?"

"She's downstairs. Uh . . . You should know that Grom is here, too."

Grom left the tribunal and headed for land? Did that mean it all ended badly? Well, even *worse* than my getting impaled? An urgent need to know everything about everything shimmies through me. "Whoa. Sit. Talk. Now."

He laughs. "I will, I promise. But I want to make you comfortable first."

"Well, then, you need to come over here and switch places with the bed." A blush fills my cheeks, but I don't care. I need him. All of him. It feels like forever since we've talked like this, just me and him. But talking usually doesn't last long. Lips were made for other things, too. And Galen is especially good at the other things.

He walks back and squats by the bed. "You have no idea how tempting that is." It seems like the violet of his eyes gets darker. It's the color they get when he has to pull away from me, when we're about to violate a bunch of Syrena laws if we don't stop. "But you're not well enough to . . ." He runs a hand through his hair. "I'll go get Rachel. Then we can talk."

I'm a little surprised that his argument didn't begin with "But the law . . ." That is what has stopped us in the past. Now the only thing that appears to be stopping us is my stabby condition.

What's changed?

And why am I not excited about it? I used to get so frustrated when he would pull away. But a small part of me loved that about him, his respect for the law and for the tradition of his people. His respect for *me*. Respect is a hard thing to come by when picking from among human boys. Is that respect gone?

And is it my fault?

After a few minutes both Mom and Rachel come to my aid. They give me pain medication and water. Then Mom announces that it's time for a shower and fresh pajamas. She helps me to the bathroom, helps me wash, then helps me put a gazillion tangles in my hair while she shampoos it. And she actually thinks we're going to leave it that way.

"I'm not going downstairs looking like a hobo," I tell her. "We have to comb it."

"That thick mess will break this flimsy comb. Can't you just run your fingers through it?"

It's weird to be arguing about my hair when we still haven't discussed my wound, how I got it, and how I came to be snoring in Galen's bed. We both seem to appreciate the bizarreness at the same time. Mom raises a brow. "Don't think you get special treatment just because you can make a whale do the tango. I'm still your mother."

We both laugh so hard I think I feel a tiny rip in my newly dressed wound. Without warning, Mom throws her arms around me, careful to avoid touching it. "I'm so proud of you, Emma. And I know your father would be, too. Your grandfather can't stop talking about it. You were amazing."

Ah, the bonding power of tangled hair and dancing whales.

She releases me the second before it gets awkward. "Let's get you dressed. We have a lot to discuss. And I bet you're starving. Rachel made you . . . uh . . . Upchuck Eggs."

"She gets an A for effort."

Mom hands me my clothes.

We find Galen and Grom sitting in the formal dining room, talking quietly to each other across the gigantic mahogany table. Steam billows up from several pots spread across it, polluting the air with the smell of seafood. Out of the sixteen glossy high-back chairs, I take the one next to Galen.

He stops his conversation with Grom and leans over to kiss my forehead. "How do you feel?"

"Hungry."

Rachel sets a plate full of eggs, jalapeños, bacon, cheese, and a bunch of other ingredients that a less-famished person might care about. I don't even blow on it before I spoon it into my mouth. As soon as I do, of course, Grom says, "Good morning, Emma."

I nod politely. "Goo monig," I tell him around my food.

Galen winks at me, then takes a bite of his own breakfast,

which looks like a crab cake the size of his face. Also, it smells like dirty socks and sauerkraut.

"Emma, we were just discussing our plans," Grom continues. "I'm glad you could join us."

I take a sip of orange juice. "Plans for what?"

Mom sits next to Grom with a cup of coffee. "Plans for living on land."

"We already live on land."

"We do," she agrees. "But it looks like we'll need to make room for a few additions to our lives." She doesn't have to look at Grom for me to know she's talking about him.

Which means everything I did was for nothing. If Grom is living on land, that means he can't return back to his territory. "They didn't believe me, then," I say. "They still took Jagen's side?"

"We don't know," Grom says. "We left right after you did, during the chaos that followed Jagen's attack. What happened after that doesn't matter. I would rather live among humans than see the ones I care about put in danger like that again."

"Me, too," Mom says, fury glinting in her eyes. "You were hurt, and I wasn't waiting around for them to throw us in the Ice Caverns for the next eternity. Idiots."

Galen places a hand on my thigh under the table and gives it a gentle squeeze. It's not meant to be sensual at all, but I've been going through Galen-withdrawals and I can't help but acknowledge the sensation of lava flowing through my veins. I try, try, try to respect that it's meant to comfort me. Galen must see it on my face because his eyes widen before he moves his hand away from me. "There's nothing for us to go back to, Emma,"

Galen says, clearing his throat. "That tribunal should have never happened. The Syrena world we once knew doesn't exist anymore."

So I was right. The only thing stopping him in the bedroom earlier was my wound. Not Syrena law. Not Syrena tradition.

"It just seems that way right now," I tell him. "Give it some time, then go back."

"No," he says. "I gave it enough time. Day after day, they didn't listen to reason. All they want is change. They don't care if it's good or bad. Now they can have it. Without the Royals."

The Syrena might need time, but Galen needs time, too. It's too soon for him to be making judgment calls like that. He's been too loyal to his kind for too long to cut them off cold-turkey. But he wouldn't appreciate me telling him so in front of his brother. Or in front of my mom. I change the subject. "Speaking of Royals, where are Rayna and Toraf? Sleeping in?"

Galen's jaw tightens. "Toraf is not welcome here. Rayna has chosen the company of her traitorous mate over the company of her family."

"Galen, Toraf isn't a traitor," I tell him gently. "He did what he did to save Rayna. To save *you*. What would have happened if I hadn't come?" But I can't convince myself that the outcome would have been different if I had opted to stay on the cozy shore. Rayna still could have—would have—saved the day.

It looks like Galen is thinking the same thing. "Then you wouldn't have been hurt," he says stubbornly. "Grom was making headway. It would have turned out fine."

"You can't be sure of that. And Toraf wasn't taking the chance."

"I'm sure he's told you some noble story. But he brought you to the Arena. He risked your life, Emma. And look what happened."

"I did what I thought was right," Toraf says from the threshold of the living room. Rayna stands behind him, indifference sheathing the nervousness I know she's probably feeling at bringing him here. Over Toraf's shoulder I see another Syrena, older and taller and lankier. I've never met him before, but I think I know who he is.

Too bad there isn't time for introductions.

Galen's abrupt stand sends his chair crashing to the floor behind him. He half-leaps, half-slides across the table, sending pots and pans and barely touched breakfasts everywhere. Within a second, he has Toraf by the neck, pinning him against the wall.

"Galen, no!" Rayna screams, beating against his back.

"Get away, Rayna," he grounds out.

Toraf takes advantage of the distraction by punching Galen in the mouth. Galen releases him, but recovers quickly, burying his fist in Toraf's gut.

Toraf swings.

Galen dances away.

Everyone at the table falls back to the wall, giving them a wide berth and the dining room as their boxing ring. Even Rayna resigns herself to the wall beside me.

"They just have to fight it out," she says, sighing.

"Until what?" I say. "Not to the death or anything stupid like that. Right?" The Syrena as a species tend to live a peaceful way of life. I can't imagine they would have a provision in their law that stipulates it's okay to fight to the death.

Except, Galen isn't concerned with the laws anymore.

Thankfully, Rayna shakes her head. "Until they're too tired to hate each other. I hate when they do this." She appears burdened with years of experiencing this.

But I can already see from the way they fight and struggle that they don't hate each other. They are not trying to kill each other. They are both hurt inside, and want to translate that into physical blows. This brawl is a conversation. An understanding. And hopefully, a healing.

"Getting tired already, minnow?" Toraf taunts as he wraps strong arms around Galen's neck in a choke hold.

Galen promptly flips him forward and onto his back. Toraf bounces once with the force. "You must have been drinking salt water," Galen returns, "to have delusions like that."

Toraf kicks Galen's legs out from under him, and the scuffle is taken to the floor. Just when I wonder how long this can really go on, the older Syrena steps into the dining room and confirms his identity with the authority in his voice. "That's enough. Get up."

Toraf scrambles to his feet and steps away from Galen, who reluctantly complies. "Yes, Highness. Sorry, Highness," Toraf says, breathless. There is not a small amount of shame on Toraf's face.

In fact, even Galen looks conscience stricken. "Apologies, King Antonis," he says quickly. "I didn't see you there."

King Antonis. Mom's dad. My grandfather. *Holy!*

Antonis lifts his chin, satisfied. "I didn't think so."

Mom steps over the dish debris and embraces her dad. "Thank you for interrupting. It was getting a tad boring. It was obvious no one would win."

Mom is such a dude sometimes. Grom winks at Galen, who shrugs.

"What brings you inland, Father?" Mom asks. "Besides the entertainment, of course."

"I've brought news," he says. "Toraf was kind enough to escort me here."

"What news?" Galen and Grom ask at the same time.

That Galen is interested in any kind of news from the Syrena world is a good sign. He's not as ready to give up on them as he thinks.

Antonis motions toward the living room. That's when I realize he's wearing a pair of Galen's swim trunks—and they're in danger of slinking to his ankles. "I assume these structures are made for sitting?"

We follow him and seat ourselves on the sectional. Rayna seats herself on Toraf's lap. We all lean in toward my grandfather. It's so weird to think of him in those terms.

"Much has happened," Antonis begins. "The commotion caused by the Gifts of Triton and the Gift of Poseidon attracted some human attention."

"Gifts?" Galen interjects. "You mean my sister's Gift of Triton. The power in her voice."

Ah. So her insane screaming fit *did* create the waves. It wasn't just my imagination. But if *that* wasn't my imagination, then Galen's fin—

"It is rude to interrupt a king," Antonis says sternly. Then his face softens. "It has come to our attention, young prince, that you, too, possess the Gift of Triton. We believe that since you are twins, the Gift was split between you. To our knowledge, this has never happened before."

Galen shakes his head. "But I don't—"

"It's your speed, squid breath," Rayna says, rolling her eyes. "Have you seen your fin lately?"

Galen mulls over this. "I've always been fast. It was never called 'the Gift' before. What's the difference now?"

"You've never been *that* fast, minnow," Toraf says. "You divided the water like a shaker divides land."

"It was most impressive," Antonis says. "As was my granddaughter." He gives me a smile bursting with pride and approval. Apparently my grandfather is no longer prejudiced against Half-Breeds, if he ever was. I wonder if this is one of those defining moments in life where a relationship starts.

And I hope it is.

"And it all makes sense, of course," Mom says.

Everyone nods knowingly. Which drives me mental. "What makes sense?" I decide they're just going to have to make concessions for me; I didn't have the luxury of growing up to Syrena fairy tales.

Grom is the first to answer. "It is thought that the Gifts only occur when there is a need. With everything going on, and the stress my brother and sister were under, the Gifts made an appearance. Rayna used it to save you. Then Galen used it to save you. The same way you used it to save them. The purpose of the Gifts is survival, after all."

It feels like the world suddenly got bigger. Awareness of

things greater than me and Galen and everyone in this room settles on me like a coating of insight dust. *The Gifts appear when needed.* The first time it appeared for me was when I was drowning in my grammy's backyard pond. I used the Gift to talk to the catfish, who pushed me to the surface. It was life or death. Just like it was life or death back at the Arena.

"Does that . . . Does that answer your question?" Galen says softly.

I nod. The room is quiet, in a sort of collective reflection. Then Grom reminds us all why my grandfather is here.

"You said humans came?" Grom says.

Antonis nods grimly. "They've captured two Syrena. The humans are holding them on the inhabited island closest to the Arena."

"Who did they take?" Grom asks.

"Jagen and a Triton Tracker, Musa. The council of Archives is requesting the help of the Gifts," Antonis says solemnly. "They recognize now that they have been gravely mistaken to doubt the Royals."

Galen scoffs. "It's a little late, don't you think? They were ready to throw us in the Ice Caverns two days ago."

"Besides that, what can we do anyway?" Rayna says. "There are only three of us with Gifts. And our Gifts don't work on land, remember? Humans have all sorts of stuff they could use on us."

"That's not true," Grom says. "Remember the story of the generals? Triton sent the big waves *to* land. He destroyed humans with it, drowned them all on their own ground."

"That was a long time ago," Mom argues. "They were practically defenseless. Humans have much more advanced methods of protecting themselves now."

"Not to mention, I'm not in a particular hurry to save Jagen," Galen says. "I'd say he got exactly what he deserved."

I'm thinking the same thing. I can't help it. The guy stabbed me.

"It would be unfair to take that perspective, brother," Grom tells him. "We are not doing it for Jagen. We are doing it for our kind."

"We?" Rayna snaps. "What Gift do you have, Grom? Oh, that's right. You and Nalia get to stay safely behind while me and Galen and Emma drown an entire island."

Oh heck no. "Um, I'm not killing anyone," I say, raising my hand. "Not humans, not Syrena."

"It's a good thing your Gift isn't deadly then, isn't it?" Rayna sneers. "I have an idea. You can give the humans their last meal. That would be special, wouldn't it?"

"How would *you* like to go without eating for a while?" I shoot back. I could use my Gift to send the fish away from her, or I could just bust all her teeth out. Maturity seems to be evaporating into the air. I wonder if her Gift includes pushing all my buttons in rapid-point-five seconds. But then, I know her animosity is really toward Grom, not me. All I'm doing is feeding her anxiety.

Galen tucks a tendril of my hair behind my ear. It's enough to distract me and he knows it. I give him a sour look for interfering, but he grins. "You don't have to kill anyone, angelfish. In fact, we need your help to *save* them." He seems to be telling me something with his eyes, but I'm not picking up on it. I'd love to blame it on the pain meds.

"Doesn't that kind of miss the point?" Rayna says.

"Of course not," Galen says. "Our objective is to rescue our kind, not kill the humans. We can do that without destroying them."

Everyone is all ears, but Galen is not ready to divulge his plan just yet. He stands. "Highness, tell the Archives we will meet with them to discuss our terms."

"Terms?" Grom says. "This isn't negotiable, Galen. They need us. It's our duty as Royals."

Galen shrugs. "As far as I'm concerned, it's entirely negotiable. And we're not Royals anymore, not until I hear it from their lips." He turns to Antonis. "And tell them that in view of recent events, the council must come here, on land. There is no reason for us to doubt that this is a trap to recapture us."

Antonis chuckles. I get the feeling that this is all an amusing game to him. But then, old people have earned the right to be amused by everything. And I'm pretty sure he's the oldest person I know.

"Young Prince Galen, I am at your service." With that, my grandfather leaves. I turn away as he begins to finagle the shorts from his skinny waist on his way down the beach.

20

GALEN STANDS behind Rachel and Emma as they scroll down the screen of the laptop. "Toraf stuck his foot in the water. The Archive council will be here soon. Antonis is with them." He's met with silence, except for Rachel flipping the page of a notebook she has in front of her. Emma bites the end of a pencil as she watches Rachel scrawl on the page. Being ignored is not Galen's favorite. "What are you doing?" he says.

Emma looks up. "Oh. Hey. We're researching that island on the Internet. Might as well do some recon while we're waiting, right?"

Brilliant. The Internet. Galen keeps forgetting that he's not without his resources, either. The humans have their technology, but Galen has it, too. Plus, he's got something better. Rachel.

"The island is called Kanton," Rachel says. "Do you want the good news, or the bad news first?"

"Bad news," Galen says.

"Everyone who lives on the island is either government employees, or the family of government employees."

"Which government?" Emma asks.

Galen taps her on the shoulder and motions for her to let him sit. Pulling her into his lap, he peers around her hair to the screen, trying to ignore her scent and failing miserably at it.

"Some country called Kiribati," Rachel says. "Never heard of it."

"Me, either," Emma says.

"What's the good news?" Galen says.

"The good news is that there are only about a dozen people living there. Not a whole lot of technology going on here like we thought. Their job is to keep the surrounding waters protected from commercial fishing. But"—Galen hates it when she says "but"—"there *is* a functioning airport on the north side. They could have already flown your friends out of there."

"Is there any way to find out if they did?" Galen says.

Rachel shrugs. "I think it's safe to assume that if the discovery of mermaids—sorry, *Syrena*—isn't all over the news by now, then probably they're still there. If your friends are smart, they'll stay in human form."

"Why would they keep a big discovery like that under wraps?" Emma says, frowning. "It would be the biggest scientific finding in centuries. Maybe ever."

"Like I said." Rachel takes a sip of her wine. "Maybe they haven't shown them what they are. Maybe they think they just rescued some dumb humans from drowning or something. That would be the best-case scenario." She snorts. "Maybe they got arrested for commercial fishing."

"Can you give us an advantage at all?" Emma asks Rachel. "Like, shut down their communications or something? Work your Rachel magic?"

Rachel shakes her head. "I can't find much about this island as it is. I'm not sure what kind of communications they have, but I'm guessing satellite phones or something. What I can do though, is create a distraction at the closest airport to them, which is . . ." Her fingers move deftly over the keys. "Puka Puka Airport in the Cook Islands. If I make landing conditions unsafe there or screw around with their flight schedule, and say, the next five closest airports around them, they won't be able to export your friends until we've had a chance to get to them. Better make the first attempt count though."

Emma nods. "We will. And did you get the life jackets we talked about?"

"Life jackets?" Galen says. He doesn't like Emma and Rachel making plans together. Not because he thinks they're being devious, but because he doesn't like feeling left out. Not to mention that when Emma is making plans without him, they're usually reckless. The only reason she'd keep a secret from him is if she was doing something he didn't approve of, or didn't want him to interfere with. After all, her motto is "Better to ask for forgiveness than permission."

Galen despises that motto.

"I cleared out the sporting goods store this morning," Rachel says. "I took what was on the shelf and made them cough up their stock in the back."

Galen tenses up. Emma laughs. "Don't be jealous, Highness. Rachel still loves you more than she loves me."

"Aww! You guys are fighting over me?" Rachel says, pinching Galen's cheek. "That's so adorable."

"I'm not jealous," he says, trying not to sound pouty. "I just don't know why we would need life jackets."

"*We* don't," Emma says, wriggling around on his lap so she can face him. Secretly, he's delighted. "But humans do. And if my job is keeping the humans safe, then I should be prepared, right?"

But Galen is too distracted by the close proximity of her mouth to be bothered with the words coming out of it. She must recognize it, because she leans forward as if giving him a chance to make good on his craving. It's all the invitation he needs.

He captures her mouth with his. Life jackets, islands, and airports are forgotten. The only thing that exists is her lips on his, her body pressed into his. Suddenly the creaky office chair is transformed into their own little world.

"Uh, I'm just going to get more wine," Rachel says. He didn't mean to make her uncomfortable enough to leave. *Not good. The last thing we need is privacy and free rein to do as we please.* He tries to end it, to pull away, but Emma won't have it. And it's difficult for him not to indulge her.

Her kiss is hungry, as if long deprived. As if they didn't already spend the morning doing just exactly this, making up for the lost time they were apart. *Triton's trident, I could do this all day.* Then he catches himself. *No, I couldn't. Not without wanting more. Which is why we need to stop.*

Instead, he entwines his hands in her hair, and she teases his lips with her tongue, trying to get him to fully open his mouth to her. He gladly complies. Her fingers sneak their way under his shirt, up his stomach, sending a trail of fire to his chest.

He is about to lose his shirt altogether. Until Antonis's voice booms from the doorway. "Extract yourself from Prince Galen, Emma," he says. "You two are not mated. This behavior is inappropriate for any Syrena, let alone a Royal."

Emma's eyes go round as sand dollars. He can tell she's not sure what to think about her grandfather telling her what to do. Or maybe she's caught off guard that he called her a Royal. Either way, like most people, Emma decides to obey. Galen does, too. They stand up side by side, not daring to be close enough to touch. They behold King Antonis in a polka-dot bathrobe, and though he's the one who looks silly, they are the ones who look shamed.

Galen feels like a fingerling again. "I apologize, Highness," he says. It seems like all he does lately is apologize to the Poseidon king. "It was my fault."

Antonis gives him a reproving look. "I like you, young prince. But you well know the law. Do not disappoint me, Galen. My granddaughter is deserving of a proper mating ceremony."

Galen can't meet his eyes. *He's right. I shouldn't be flirting with temptation like this.* With the Archives on their way—or possibly here already—there is a distant but small chance that he and Emma can still live within the confines of the law. That they can still live as mates under the Syrena tradition. And he almost just blew it. *What if it had gone too far?* Then his mating with Emma would forever be blemished by breaking the law. "It won't happen again, Highness." *Not until we're mated, anyway.*

"Um. Did you just promise not to kiss me ever again?" Emma whispers.

"Can we talk about this later? The Archives are obviously here, angelfish."

She's on the verge of a fit, he can tell. "He's just looking out for us," Galen says quickly. "I agree, we need to respect the law—"

At this her fit subsides as if it was never there. She smiles wide at him. He can't decide if it's genuine, or if it's the kind of smile she gives him when he'll pay for something later. "Okay, Galen."

"Galen, Emma," Nalia calls from the dining room, saving him from making a fool of himself. "Everyone is here."

Emma gives him a look that clearly says "We're so not done with this conversation." Then she turns and walks away. Galen takes a second to regain a little bit of composure—which kissing Emma tends to steal from him. Then there's the mortification of being interrupted by— *Get it together, idiot.*

Galen uses the walk to the dining room to settle his nerves and stifle the anger building up inside him. The truth is, he doesn't have much to say to the Archives. Not after what they allowed to take place in the Arena. *Triton's trident, they put the Royals on trial!*

But as much as Galen would love to throw that in their faces, he won't. This is his one chance, however small it is, to turn things around for him and Emma. And he's not about to toss that chance to sea with both hands.

Rachel has pulled more chairs out to accommodate the gathering. The table they circle is shinier than Emma's lip gloss. Unlike the human meetings Galen has attended with Rachel to sell his underwater finds, there is no paperwork on the table, no cups of coffee, no cell phones. Also unlike human meetings, most participants are either dressed in bathing suits or bathrobes. *Leave it to Rachel's creative hospitality.* It is a sight Galen will never forget, seeing the elderly council of Archives sit uncomfortably in human chairs. If the situation weren't so dire, he'd have to laugh. Especially since Tandel's bathrobe has the human symbol of peace all over it in fluorescent colors.

"Thank you for coming," Galen says. He takes his place next to Grom, who sits at the head of the table. Appropriately, Antonis sits at the head of the other end, accompanied by Rayna and Toraf. Emma is at Galen's left side. He doesn't need to look at her to know she's scowling at him.

Grom begins. "King Antonis has been so kind as to give us your message and deliver ours. Many thanks to you, Highness."

Antonis nods, bored.

"We would very much like to hear what you have to say to us," Grom continues. "Have you elected someone to speak on behalf of the council?"

Tandel raises his hand. Galen is not surprised. "I have been elected, Majesty."

Grom nods at him, and Tandel's face changes from nervous to apologetic. "First, I would like to express on behalf of all of us here—and many who are not—that we are terribly sorry for the way the tribunal was handled." When none of the Royals accept nor reject his offering of remorse, Tandel continues, less confident. "In fact, we regret that there was a tribunal at all. We had no right to question the actions of the Royals. It was shameful that we allowed Jagen to tickle our ears with such nonsense."

"Nonsense?" Galen interrupts. He would like Tandel to be much more specific. After all, the more guilt that can be piled on the Archives' heads, the better chance Galen has of getting what he wants.

Tandel nods. "The nonsense that a Common could have the Gift of Poseidon." Galen does not miss his quick glance at Emma. "Paca has come forward and admitted her guilt in this conspiracy. It was just as you said, King Grom. She learned the hand signals from the humans while she was on land."

"And what of Nalia?" Grom says, motioning to her on his other side. "What conclusion has the council reached regarding her?"

"There are still those who claim that they do not recognize her pulse, Highness. However," Tandel adds quickly at Grom's immediate scowl, "we must assume that since Jagen and Paca lied about so much, that some of their Loyals did as well, and continue to do so. It has come to the attention of the council that Jagen offered many positions of prominence in his new 'kingdom' arrangement. It is our belief that he intended to change our entire way of life."

Grom folds his hands on the table. "And?"

"We are prepared to accept the blue-eyed Syrena as Nalia, the Poseidon heir. After all, we do have testimony from well-respected Trackers and Archives who insist she is who she says."

"You well know that I only mated with Paca because I thought she had the Gift of Poseidon. What of that?"

"I'm not sure I understand what you're asking, Highness."

"I'm quite certain that you are quite certain of what I'm

asking. You know I was promised to Nalia before the mine explosion. You know I mated with Paca under false pretenses. And you know that we have not consummated the bond."

Tandel sighs. "Your mating with Paca is legal, Highness. We have no grounds for dissolving the union. The only grounds for dissolution is adultery."

"Then why did you come here?" Rayna says. "You knew what we were going to ask of you. Why else would we care if Nalia was the Poseidon heir or not? So she could float around all useless? She's supposed to be with my brother. You have a lot of nerve—"

"That's enough, Rayna," Grom says. Before her feelings have time to get hurt, he adds, "Thank you for making those excellent points." Galen has noticed that since Nalia is back, Grom has been more patient with Rayna. It occurs to Galen that maybe Rayna reminded his brother of Nalia so much that he kept her at a distance all this time. After all, they share much the same spirit of rebellion and adventure. The revelation makes Galen smile.

Grom turns his attention to Tandel expectantly.

"Is this what you ask in exchange for your help?" Tandel asks.

Grom is about to confirm that it is, but Galen stops him. "No," he says forcefully. "That is only one of the things we're asking."

Grom's eyes widen, but he allows Galen to speak. "You have not only broken the law by your treasonous tribunal. You're breaking the law right now, sitting here in a structure made by human hands and clothes made for humans to wear. Tell me why you break the law right now."

Tandel is getting flustered. "You yourself requested our presence here, Highness."

"And you agreed. Why did you agree?"

"We came to address an issue that affects our kind."

"So you overlooked the law to make this concession. For the greater good of all Syrena."

Tandel nods reluctantly. "That is one way of putting it, Highness."

Galen leans forward, folds his hands on the table carefully. He takes care to look into the eyes of each Archive. He takes care to let them know he is talking to each of them, and all of them as a council. "I will ask you to do it again."

"I beg your pardon, Majesty?" Tandel says.

"I will ask you to break the law once again, for the greater good of all Syrena." The words are out of his mouth but he can't tell if they made their mark.

Especially because of the outbreak of gasps—not the least of which is from Grom. But Grom should have seen this coming. He was so quick to look out for his own desires, that he forgot what Galen wanted. The *only* thing Galen wanted. When things quiet down, Galen continues. "You have made the acquaintance of Emma, Half-Breed daughter of Nalia. All of you witnessed that she has the true Gift of Poseidon, that she is a direct descendant of the General himself. And you should know that I intend to take her as my mate."

Galen allows the room to transfer the shock among themselves. Across the table, Antonis nods to him in approval from the comfort of his purple polka-dot bathrobe. The act seems to empower Galen, to infuse him with boldness. He waits for Tandel to resume eye contact with him.

"Prince Galen, this is a surprise to us all. We expected you to request that we allow her to live, though she is a Half-Breed. In view of her efforts to save the fingerling Jasa from humans, we were prepared to concede to that."

I'd almost forgotten that. And so far, Emma hasn't come forward and confessed that she was in the water *when he'd asked* her not to be. That she allowed herself to be seen by a stranger, even if just a fingerling.

Galen whips his glare to Emma. Her face is red, painted with guilt. "Did you forget to mention something to me?" he hisses.

"Oh. Yeah. About that. We have a lot to talk about *later*, don't we?" she whispers.

Tandel clears his throat. "What you are suggesting, what you are asking, is not conceivable, Highness. Because of Nalia's reappearance and Grom's recent mating ceremony to Paca, you do realize you are in line to mate with the Poseidon heir. You are a Royal, Prince Galen. A Royal has no business mating with a Half-Breed."

Galen was afraid this would happen. That he really would be forced to choose. Before, when they had wronged him and the rest of the Royals, it was an easy decision to make. Now the Archives seek reconciliation. They seek negotiations. Will Galen be the one to reopen the closing chasm between the Royals and the Archives?

Galen is about to respond, but Grom beats him to it. "Just like a Royal has no business mating with a Common, Tandel? It seems my brother is right. The Archives are willing to negotiate the rules when it suits them. Thus far, the Royals have not negotiated. Every third generation for as long as can be remembered, the Royals have sacrificed their own desires and joined the two houses, just as the law requires. We have given much, and you have rewarded our sacrifice with disloyalty. Betrayal." Grom holds his hand when it looks like Tandel might interrupt. Or apologize again. "No, let me speak. You yourselves saw the Gift Emma possesses. I would think you would *want* to keep that Gift within the bloodlines. Can you imagine what their fingerlings could do, coming from parents who each have a Gift of the generals? Aside from that, I was under the impression that you were asking for Emma's help with the humans as well? If so, this is not the way to go about it, friends. It seems to me that as far as Half-Breeds go, this is one you'd want to become an ally of. Not to mention, this would very much go against my own wishes. You know my reasoning for wanting to unseal my mating with Paca. To have my brother mate with Nalia instead would hardly encourage affection among the Royals."

Galen can't think of anything else he would add to Grom's argument. In fact, he probably wouldn't have been as eloquent; he was about to call the entire thing off and send them back to where they came from. Which is why it is a very good thing that Grom is king instead of Galen.

More scattered whispers echo off the walls and the bamboo flooring. Galen wonders that they get anything accomplished at all, if they handle all affairs with such disorganization. After a while, Tandel calls for silence and stands. "If it pleases the Royals, the council would like to convene outside in private. These are not small requests we are taking into consideration, and they are more than we had anticipated."

Grom nods. "Of course. But keep in mind that while you deliberate, humans have two of our kind. That is not a small thing, either."

When the Archives file out of the room, Galen turns to Emma. She's ready for him. She holds up her shushing finger. "Don't even," she says. "I was going to tell you, but I just didn't have a chance."

"Tell me now," he says. "Since it seems I'm the last to know." He isn't the last to know, of course. But he'd really hoped she would come to him with it. Before now. Before it became an issue for other people.

She raises a hesitant brow.

"*Please*," he grates out.

She sighs in a gust. "I still don't think it's important at the moment, but when Rayna took off for the Arena, I hopped on one of the jet skis and tried to follow. But," she amends, "I did not intend to get in the water. I swear I didn't. It's just that Goliath wanted to play, and he tipped over the"—she must sense all his patience oozing out—"anyway, so I come across this Syrena, Jasa, and she's been caught in a net and two men are pulling her aboard. So me and Goliath helped her."

"Where are the fishermen now?"

"Um. Unless Rachel did something drastic, they're probably at home telling their kids crazy stories about mermaids."

Galen feels a sense of control slipping, but of what he's not sure. For centuries, the Syrena have remained unnoticed by humans. Now within the span of a week, they've allowed themselves to be captured twice. He hopes this does not become a pattern.

Toraf must have mistaken his long pause for brooding. "Don't be too hard on her, Galen," he says. "I told you, Emma helped her and then went straight home."

"Stay out of this," Galen says pleasantly.

"I *knew* you told him." Emma crosses her arms at Toraf. "You really are a snitch."

"You had enough to worry about. And so did I." Toraf shrugs, unperturbed. "It's over now."

Nalia pinches the bridge of her nose. "This is where I ground you for life," she tells Emma. "All three hundred years of it."

It looks like Emma might be about to correct her mother, to tell her what Dr. Milligan told them about the reduced life span of a Half-Breed. Galen shakes his head at her amid the sick feeling he always gets when he remembers he will outlive her. There's no reason to bring this up now. There will be plenty of time to sort out all the details of the past few months soon enough.

Which is what Emma is trying to tell me about helping Jasa. "Fine," Galen says. "It's fine. You did what you had to do."

The rest of their wait is spent in silence. Galen tries to read his brother's expression, but as usual, Grom has his emotions hidden away under the layers of nonchalance. Toraf and Rayna seem to be playing some sort of game with each other under the table and Antonis appears utterly bored. Emma stares thoughtfully at the wall behind her mother, at the painting of a lighthouse on a windy day. Galen wonders what she's thinking. But since this could be the calm before the tempest, depending on what the Archives decide, he lets her daydream and have her peace.

"Excuse me, Highness," Tandel calls from the doorway. "But we have come to a conclusion."

Galen notices that the other Archives did not rejoin their speaker, which means they're all in agreement about their decision. They did not debate very long at all. Which could be good or bad.

"So that we are of the same mind, King Grom, I would like to take the time to restate the terms of your return to power, and your assistance in helping us retrieve our lost."

"Please do."

Tandel bows. "Thank you, Majesty. Now, it is our understanding that his Majesty Grom is requesting an unsealing from his mating with the Common Paca?"

"That is correct," Antonis says, rolling his eyes. "Poseidon's beard, but this is repetitive."

Tandel ignores the elder king's bluster. "It is also our understanding that Prince Galen requests, in exchange for his help, and the help of Emma the Half-Breed, that he is permitted to mate with Emma as if she were full-blooded Syrena."

"You have that correct," Galen answers gruffly.

Tandel pauses. "And do the Royals have any more requests at this time?"

"Yes," Emma says, to Galen's surprise. She's never held back from speaking what's on her mind. But she never acknowledged herself as a Royal until now. "Because of my Half-Breed status, and the fact that I've lived on land all my life, I would like for the Royals to be able to visit me here whenever they like. I know that under the current laws, that's not allowed, but I want that changed."

"You might as well agree to that, Tandel," Antonis says. "Or else you'll be holding another tribunal for the Royals, because all of us intend to be visiting land more often I think."

"Actually, I won't be visiting land," Galen says. He turns to Emma. "I'll be living here." Tears pool in her eyes. He catches one sliding down her cheek and kisses it away. Her reaction just confirms what he'd suspected all along. That she's been worried about it. How it would work out between them, where would they live. Emma had said before that she wanted the best of both worlds. Prom, graduation, college. Swimming with dolphins, visiting the *Titanic*, searching for Amelia Earhart's plane. He intends to make sure she has it all.

Tandel sighs. "I had a feeling you might say that, Prince Galen. I did not really see it working any other way. So, I already proposed the possibility of that request to the council as well." Galen wasn't requesting it, he was simply informing Tandel of what he was going to do. But he decides not to correct the old Archive. Being overly stubborn on matters would only leave a sour taste in the council's mouth. Not only against him, but against all the Royals. If the council perceives their requests as burdensome, it will only be a matter of time before another conflict arises.

Of course, this last tribunal of the Royals will have a rippling effect on generations to come. Others may seek out the weaknesses or imperfections in their leaders, because they saw how close Jagen came to succeeding. How things are dealt with today will affect the image of the Royals from now on. And Jagen has shown them the value in maintaining appearances.

"Please know it was an unanimous decision," Tandel continues. "We have heard your logic. While we feel some of your requests are not in the best interest of the law, we all agree that they are in the best interest of the *spirit* of the law, which is, and always has been, the unity and survival of our kind. As a council, we recognize that the world around us is changing, and that we must find new ways to adapt and change with it. We feel that what you are requesting is not unreasonable. And we will concede." Before everyone gets too excited though, Tandel holds up his hand. "However, it must be stated that the consideration we are showing Emma—and Prince Galen—is an isolated matter. We still stand by the law forbidding Half-Breeds, as we feel it is for our protection not to become so entangled in the human world. Emma is the only exception, and if not for her previous show of concern for her Syrena heritage, we would decline this particular request. This special provision will be forever recorded in our history, in our collective memories as Archives."

Emma looks like she wants to disagree, but Galen places a hand on her leg and shakes his head. Now is not the time to debate these things. Now is the time to accept small victories and take what they can get. Not to mention, he agrees with the Archives on that particular point. Some humans can be trusted. Most cannot.

Emma puts her hand on his and squeezes it in understanding. Her cheeks fill with a blush of what he hopes is excitement. They can be together. Legally.

"Now it's our turn to meet the terms of the negotiation, right?" Rayna says, standing and stretching. "Let's get on with it."

21

RAYNA, GALEN, Toraf, and I swim several loops around the island of Kanton to become familiar with the area. There's an inland lagoon full of all kinds of fish species, which will make my job ten times easier. The seven or so Trackers who have kept watch tell us that so far, no one has left the island and no one has come in—a good sign.

Rachel had a fabulous time screwing with flight schedules and such. Soon she should be arriving by boat with the life jackets. Galen and I make it clear to the Trackers that she is not the enemy.

"She's going to spread them all over the place," Galen tells them. "Our goal is to rescue Jagen and Musa. We do not want human casualties."

But some of the Trackers look like maybe they do want human casualties. I can't blame them. Right now, they perceive the humans as villains. As a threat. Still, if they can't control their anger, they aren't of any use to us. "If you're not going to help, then you're going to be in the way," I say. "Decide now which it will be."

They don't seem to like my giving them orders. Toofreakingbad, I want to tell them. Two of the Trackers actually do leave, and it makes me want to sic some sharks on them, just as a scare tactic. *So much for feeling compassionate.*

One of the remaining Trackers glides closer to me. "Emma, daughter of Nalia, granddaughter of Antonis. I am Kana, Jasa's mother. I want to thank you for helping her escape the fishermen's net. I am indebted to you."

"You can pay your debt here today," I tell her solemnly, which makes me feel a little cheesy. "By helping save human lives."

In the distance, we hear the thrum of a boat. Rachel signals her arrival by dumping piles of life jackets on the surface. She makes her planned circle around the island, leaving a trail of dissipating wake on the surface. The life jackets land with muted plops. Soon, and as expected, we hear the thrum of a second boat.

I watch as they converge on each other. Rachel shuts off her engine. My eyes meet Galen's. This is all according to plan, which means the plan is happening. We are really doing this. The other boat's motor remains a constant thrum. We anticipated that Rachel would get pulled over by one of the patrolling boats; since they're probably policing for potential commercial fishermen in the area, her little stunt will be an unexpected diversion.

Galen and I surface quietly behind Rachel's vessel to eavesdrop. Even if we don't learn anything critical to our cause, I already know the exchange will be full of entertainment value.

The two-man crew of the patrol boat does not speak English. Rachel exploits this as best she can, while still dumping life jackets in the water. "What? I don't understand what you're saying? Do you speak English?"

They confirm in their native tongue that they obviously do not. Rachel must be putting on a theatrical display, because the small boat rocks while she talks. "I don't need these life jackets anymore," she says, in her thickest Italian accent. "The colors are all wrong for me. I mean, look at this orange. Ew, right?"

Galen rolls his eyes. I try not to giggle.

"And this green? Hideous!" she continues.

The men get more irate when she doesn't stop littering their domain. "Hey, what the . . . Don't touch me! I have a foot I injury, you jerk!"

Galen and I slink below the surface. "We knew that might happen," he says. More accurately, we were hoping it would. If Rachel is on a boat with other humans, they'll feel obligated to look after her safety. Plus, that's two humans we can count on who won't be on the island when it floods. Two human lives we don't have to worry about. If Rachel's estimates are correct, that leaves ten left to look for.

Galen glances up at the belly of Rachel's abandoned boat. "So now they've got Rachel in custody. Make sure to keep an eye out for her when we flood the island. Her cast is going to make it next to impossible for her to swim, in the event that the boat tips." But we're really hoping the patrolmen will stay away from the waves. Right now they're moving in the opposite direction of the island, probably looking for more boats in the area who might be conspiring with Rachel.

"Will do. I think it's time to go ahead and start, don't you? We don't want them to have enough time to make a trip back to shore with her."

Galen swims to within an inch of my face. His lazy grin sends a thousand butterflies whipping up a tornado in my stomach. "Start what? The rescue, or the rest of our lives together?"

Just the words make my heart jump, let alone the look he gives me when he says it. We haven't had much time to talk about what all this means for us, but at least I know we can be together. On our own terms, in our own time. Finally. "Both," I breathe.

"This is not the time to be all mushy," Rayna calls from below us. "I swear you two are expert time wasters. So inconsiderate."

Galen winks at me and dives to his sister.

"Wait," I call to him. He stops. "I just wanted to say, I like your big fin. I think it's sexy." Which is the truth. Now it's more than double the size of any other Syrena. I know he's self-conscious about it; he thinks it makes him stand out more. What Galen doesn't realize is that he already stood out. He was already special. This new fin doesn't change anything. Well, except for making me hotter for him than I already was.

"Really?" Galen says.

I nod and blow him a kiss. By his confused expression, he has no idea what I'm doing. My Syrena human ambassador still has a lot to learn about the intimate details of the human world. And I'll be happy to assist him with that.

Rayna makes a face as he wraps his arms around her waist.

I know she's nervous, even if she won't admit it. They've only practiced this once on the way here, on a smaller scale. Rayna's voice is like a tuning fork. At the right level, it's capable of destruction. After we told Dr. Milligan what happened at the Arena, he said he wouldn't doubt that her power is sonar based—which means we may attract a different kind of human attention. Rachel said human governments keep track of sonar disturbances.

And since Rayna doesn't have her Gift completely under control yet, we're taking a risk by showing up on someone's radar. But this is the best option we've got. We all agreed that she wouldn't go all out, that she would put just enough force to flood the island. We're not going for a catastrophic event here. We're looking to give Jagen and Musa a small advantage. If we can raise the water level enough, they can swim out faster than the humans can catch them.

If they're still here, that is.

"Ready when you are," Galen tells his sister.

At this, Rayna opens her big fat mouth and screams. The result is instantaneous and huge. It looks like a wall of sound rushing away from them toward the shallow water. Galen swims faster, clutching his sister in his arms. Together, with the combination of speed and sound, they make their way around the island, producing baby-sized waves at first. When they gain momentum, the waves get bigger, travel faster, and pull some of the shallow water into the deep. I wasn't there to see Triton destroy Tartessos all those years ago. These waves cannot possibly be as big as Triton's were. I can only imagine what it would be like to stand on shore and see literal waves of destruction speeding toward you.

It would be incredible. And excessively scary.

Once the waves get into a rhythm, smacking against shore and raising the sea level, it's time for my Gift to come into play. I circle the island, making a larger ring than Galen and Rayna had made, to stay outside their range of destruction. Thankfully, the waters surrounding Kanton are a seafood buffet waiting to happen. I can definitely see why commercial fishermen would risk their licenses or arrest to get in on this. I find dolphins, whales, sharks, eels, and gigantic tuna. As I pass, I gather the larger fish to my forces. The smaller ones I send out to recruit more help, including some dolphins, since they are best at communicating with one another, and can bring friends in quickly.

"Come with me," I tell them, just like I did when I gathered my army on the way to the Boundary. "Stay close to shore and watch for humans," I keep repeating. "When the land becomes water, help the humans stay at the surface."

Gradually, the deep becomes the shallow and the shallow the deep, as the waves pummel the island. Galen and Rayna keep passing by me in a blur. Soon enough, there is no shore. There is no island. And I begin to see human legs strike the water.

"Go, go, go!" I tell my fish friends. "Guide them to the colorful things floating at the surface."

At first there are not many. It occurs to me that we could be on the wrong side of the island. I instruct the Trackers to split up, and gauge the need on the opposite side. We find the most humans on the north side, a bit more inland than I'd thought. The Trackers and I supplement the efforts of the dolphins and sharks.

I realize belatedly that sending sharks to the aid of humans is a stupid idea. When one of the men tries to kick a tiger shark in the eye—and how could I blame him?—I tell the sharks to retreat. They've done all they can do, and I won't let them be abused for their efforts.

After a few more minutes, I see a small, chubby pair of legs struggling nearby. The owner of the legs can't be older than a toddler. I scoop him up and keep him at the surface. He's adorable really, with rounded cheeks and a snotty nose and brown eyes with lashes that would make a supermodel jealous. Close to us, a woman who I assume is his mother is crying frantically and calling out to the empty waves around her. I swim him over to her and deliver the little guy into her arms. "He swallowed a good part of the ocean, but otherwise he'll be fine," I tell her, knowing that she doesn't understand.

She clutches him to her and trembles. I swim two life jackets over to her and help her strap them on to her and the baby boy. She nods, and despite the language barrier, I can tell that she's thanking me. Which makes me feel like zoo dirt, since I helped put her and her child in this predicament. If she knew that, she would probably be trying to choke the life from me. And I would probably let her.

Rachel and I didn't anticipate any children here. We were under the impression it was strictly a government facility. After all, an island isolated from the rest of the world isn't a safe place to bring your family, right? But what if we underestimated the population? What if there are more children? If any of them die, or even get injured, I'm going to hate myself. *I should have thought this through better.* Panic begins to settle in.

I dive under and try not to think about it, try to convince myself we're still doing the right thing. I pull Kana aside. "How are we doing? Any sign of Jagen or Musa? Are all the humans okay?"

That's when I realize that there aren't just Trackers around us. There are other Syrena, too. A dozen, at least. I watch in awe as they swim to the surface, find themselves a human, and keep them afloat. For every human, there is at least two watchful Syrena here to help. And there are no more pairs of stubby toddler legs.

My conscience feels rinsed with relief. I cover my mouth to stifle the overwhelming urge to bawl my eyes out.

Kana clasps my shoulder, smiling kindly. "It is not in our nature to harm humans," she explains. "We are respectful of all life, no matter to whom the life belongs. You have proven to us that you feel the same. We will help you, Emma the Half-Breed."

The number of Syrena swells beyond one hundred. We all surround the island, which is now about ten feet under water, taking turns holding humans up. Most of the humans can swim, but some of the men have on heavy boots and we have to fight with them to remove them. But a lost boot is a good trade for a saved life; some of the men see our logic, others don't.

When I'm starting to feel overconfident about our position, I take a sudden kick to the back. Which is completely my fault; I wasn't watching where I was going and got within swimming distance of a human pair of legs. It's much easier to keep your bearings when you can sense others around you. Humans don't have that luxury.

Accident or not, it feels like I've been stabbed all over again. I cry out, and swim to the surface. Kana joins me. "You're hurt?" she says.

Gritting my teeth, I nod. "It's where Jagen speared me in the back." I'm teetering on the verge of tears and I feel like such a wuss. Who am I to be crying when all these people just got displaced from their homes? No one. That's who.

I wave Kana away. "Go. Help the humans. I'll be fine." And I will be. The pain subsides and I get back to work—more carefully this time. My movements are more delicate and precise now. I'm not unaware that the tape on my bandage has come loose, that blood has started seeping out of my freshly torn wound. I'm hoping the sharks I sent away care more about my instructions than they do about the stimulating scent lingering around me.

It sucks to be a klutz on land *and* a klutz in the water.

For all our hard work, there is still no sign of Jagen or Musa. Galen glides to my side. "We think they're locked inside one of the buildings. Trackers can sense them, but we can't see them. I'm going in to get them."

"I'm coming, too."

"No, you're not. Jagen already tried to kill you once. I won't be giving him a second opportunity. Besides, we need you out here to control the marine life." Galen eyes the thin cloud of blood hovering around me like some creepy aura. Really, the blood itself is hardly visible. But I'm hyperaware of it because the water carries a faint metallic taste. I wonder how much stronger it is to Galen's full Syrena senses. I can tell he's reliving the moment I got stabbed.

He needs to snap out of it.

"I've already sent most of the fish away, what with the help of all the Syrena volunteers. The fish aren't much of a factor to our mission anymore." But I can tell by his clenched jaw and the hard look in his eyes that he's not going to budge. I am staying behind. "Take others with you, then," I say. "Jagen isn't your best friend, either."

"No, but I am," Toraf says, swimming up to us. "What are we doing?" Mom and Grom follow close behind him. I guess this is a family affair after all.

Galen shifts his glare from me to Toraf. "We're going inside the building to find Jagen and Musa. Do you sense them?"

Toraf nods. "I know exactly where they are. Follow me."

Galen presses a quick kiss to my forehead then swims after Toraf. Mom slips behind me. "Your bandage is gone. Looks like your wound might have reopened a bit."

I try to shrug casually, but wince at the shooting pain. Mom releases a sigh full of have-it-your-way. I ignore it and the tenderness in my back and the tension building in my shoulders as I watch Galen and Toraf and three other Trackers approach the submerged island.

For a government facility, the dwellings here are little more than white shacks with blinds. Which means they'll probably have to rebuild everything. I make a mental note to have Rachel send them some relief supplies when this is over.

Rachel. Ohmysweetgoodness, where is Rachel?

22

TORAF CIRCLES the building, alert, wary, and something else Galen can't quite place. "They're both still in there," Toraf says. By now, even Galen can sense the pulses of Jagen and Musa. Which means they're still alive. *So why haven't they come out yet?*

Woden, a Poseidon Tracker, slips up next to Galen. "It's been very quiet in there since the flooding started."

Toraf nods. "They can sense us as well as we can sense them. They know we're here." He turns to Galen. "What do you think?"

Galen scratches the back of his neck. "It's a trap."

Toraf rolls his eyes. "Oh, you think so?" He shakes his head. "I'm asking if you think Musa is in on it."

Galen is not very familiar with Musa. He's only talked to her a handful of times, and that was when he was very young. Still, out of all the Archives who seemed to support Jagen and his monumental act of treason, Musa's face does not come to mind. "Would she be?"

Toraf shrugs. Woden scowls. "With much respect, Highness, Musa is an Archive. She will not forsake her vows to remain neutral."

It takes all of Galen's willpower to bite his tongue. Woden is still naive enough to believe that all the Archives are of a pure and unbiased mind. That they do not get tangled up in emotions such as greed, ambition, and envy. *Did Woden attend the same tribunal I did?*

Toraf slaps Woden on the back. "Then you don't mind going first?"

The Poseidon Tracker visibly swallows. "Oh. Of course not. I'm happy to—"

"Oh, let's get on with this," Galen says, snatching the spear from Woden's unsuspecting grasp. This seems to embarrass the young Tracker. Galen doesn't have time for embarrassment.

"Yes, let's," Toraf says. "Before the humans get those disgusting wrinkles on their skin." He nudges Woden. "It's probably the most horrific thing I've ever seen. And I've seen lots of things."

It's the first time Galen realizes that Woden's nervous demeanor and over-respectful attitude is not out of reverence for his own Royal status, but out of reverence for Toraf. It seems Toraf has a fan. And why wouldn't he? He's the best Tracker in the history of both territories. Any Tracker should feel humbled in his presence.

Galen is not any Tracker. He grunts. "Shut up, idiot. Get behind me."

Toraf speeds ahead. "No, you get behind me, minnow."

Despite their grand words, they creep to the door together. Toraf presses his ear against the crackled white paint. He signals to Galen that each pulse is on opposite sides of the building. If Musa really is in on a trap, this would be a good strategy. To come at them from both sides.

They wait several more seconds, listening for any small sound, any echo of movement inside. Toraf shakes his head.

Galen nods to Woden. The young Tracker rears back and throws his weight behind his shoulder as he rams into the door. It gives immediately.

Galen's instinct is that Jagen made it too easy to enter. Not locking the door is practically an invitation. Sure, it's unlikely Jagen would even have experience with using a human lock. But given the circumstances—that Jagen's rescue is more of a capture and by now he probably knows it—Galen is sure he would have at least blocked the entrance. He isn't foolish enough to flee; he obviously accepts that Galen would catch him within seconds. But that he's desperate enough to stay, to take his chances with whoever comes through the door . . . Not good.

"Get down!" Galen yells. But Woden is already down.

So the harpoon meant for Woden hits Toraf instead. It catches his side and tears through it, almost turning him around in place. Jagen has planned well; he has obviously scavenged for as many weapons as he could find. The old harpoon gun is replaced by another one—and it's aimed to strike Galen through the heart. The close range guarantees instant death.

That is, if Jagen had time to release it. Galen slams into him, the harpoon shooting with a *pft* into the thatch roof. Together, they crash into the back wall of the building as one mass. The wood creaks, flimsy against the blunt force. All around them the frame of the building moans, threatening to collapse on them. It has already taken a battering from the waves Galen and Rayna made. It won't last much longer.

But Galen doesn't care.

Jagen almost succeeds in wresting control of the harpoon, but Galen gives it a vicious twist and presses the rod to the traitor's throat. If Jagen were human, it would cut off his air.

And Jagen's age is already telling. Galen is able to hold the harpoon rod against him with one hand. With the other, he reaches for the human utility belt strapped around Jagen's waist. Jagen squirms away, but Galen is able to grab the knife from its Velcro holster.

Jagen's eyes go wide as oysters. "You wouldn't. The law—"

"The law?" Galen snarls. "Now you want to hide behind the law? You must be joking." Out of the corner of his eye, Galen catches a glimpse of a human man tied to a chair behind the desk. Long dead. Guilt picks at his conscience like scavengers on a carcass. Did the waves kill him? Or did Jagen? But he won't—can't—give Jagen the luxury of a second glance. The human is already dead. There is nothing he can do about it now. Except . . .

Galen raises the blade above him.

Jagen closes his eyes. His trembling body suddenly sags, the harpoon the only thing holding his chin up.

The knife comes down, swift and sure and angry. With decisive, fluid movements, the human belt is off Jagen's waist, and tied around his wrists. The blade clinks to the floor with finality. If only it really were over. "If Toraf dies," Galen growls, cinching the belt to a painful tight, "I swear I'll drag your body to the Tomb Chamber myself."

Jagen nearly crumbles with relief. *He doesn't deserve relief. He deserves to be afraid. He deserves to pay for all the pain he's caused me and my family.* Galen is startled from his fury by Grom's pulse. His brother is on the other side of the room, helping Woden untie Musa from some netting. In all truthfulness, Galen had forgotten about her. He'd been so focused on Jagen and Toraf that—

"Toraf," Galen blurts.

Grom nods. "He'll be fine. Rayna is tending to him. Nalia said his organs weren't hit, but he's in and out of consciousness because he's lost a lot of blood. He's in good spirits."

Of course he is. He's probably in a state of glee right now, hoarding all of Rayna's attention to himself. Galen almost cracks a grin, but something about Grom's expression is not right. Securing the building is not the job of a Triton king. There are plenty of Trackers and hunters who can just as easily—and with less risk—help Musa from her bindings. *Why is Grom here?*

Galen swallows the bile as Woden tugs Jagen from his grasp. "Emma? Is she—"

Grom tucks his hands behind his back. "Emma is uninjured, Galen." The delicate way he swims toward Galen. As if Galen is a bubble and Grom is a lionfish. The way his mouth pulls down, as if fishing weights were hooked to each corner, tugging his mouth into a grimace. The tortured way his eyes search Galen's. As if he's asking Galen to say the words so that he doesn't have to.

"Tell me," Galen says, breathless.

Grom clasps Galen on the shoulder and gives it a gentle

squeeze. "I'm so sorry, Galen. We didn't realize they brought her back to the island. We thought she was safe on the boat."

"No," Galen whispers, backing away from the stricken Triton king. "No."

"We found her a few buildings over. The humans locked her in a room with bars. She couldn't . . ."

Galen clenches his teeth. "Not Rachel. Not Rachel." The room seems to cave in on him, or at least that's how it feels. *No, not the room. Not this insignificant room with its fragile, exhausted frame. The whole world. The whole world, with its life cycles and seasons and tides, is caving in. The whole world is pressing in on me. All of it. On my chest. So heavy.*

"The boat was headed in the opposite direction. *Away* from the island. I saw it myself."

Grom sighs. "It must have returned during all the confusion. Maybe they came back to help and didn't know what to do with her?"

Galen nods, closing his eyes. He will probably never have the answer. He will never know how Rachel came to be imprisoned on the island while he and his sister flooded it. While he and his sister sent wave after wave to drown her.

He shoves his fist in his mouth and screams into it. Then he screams again. And again. Grom keeps his distance, his hands laced together in front of him, useless in so many ways. Galen stops, holds his own hands in front of them. He examines them, scrutinizes them. *It's not fair that I call Grom's hands useless when these hands did nothing to save Rachel. They couldn't even prevent Toraf from getting hurt. Or Emma.*

"Don't do that, little brother. Don't blame yourself."

Galen's laugh is sharp, bitter. "Did I ever tell you how we met?"

Grom shakes his head almost indiscernibly.

"I saved her," Galen says, nearly choking on the words. "From drowning. Ironic, isn't it?"

"Calling it ironic is like saying she was always meant to drown. Don't read too much into it, Galen. Be kind to yourself."

"What does that even mean, Grom? Do you even know? What, I should try not to think about her if the memory is too painful? Is that how you survived all these years without Nalia?" As soon as he says the words he wants to snatch them back, to hide them back in his heart, in his serrated heart where vicious things like that shouldn't even exist. "I'm sorry, Grom. I—"

"Take a moment to compose yourself. We'll be waiting at the surface for you." Grom slinks toward the door, but pauses at the threshold. He turns back to his brother. "I am very sorry, little brother."

Galen watches as Grom propels himself out of the room. He's not sure if it was his words or his actions that took the vitality out of the normally confident stroke of Grom's fin. Probably both.

Galen closes his eyes. *How much more can I take?*

23

I KNOW the expression on Galen's face. Not because I've ever seen it before on him, but because I've had the same look. The same feelings lurking behind the expression.

First, your mind is blown. You can't accept that this person who was just with you at breakfast is now dead. She is floating in his arms, and he is gently stroking her cheek as if somehow her eyes will flutter open. Sometimes the waves nudge her head, so it looks like she moved. But she didn't.

Soon, the memories of her will flood him. Their normal daily routine, the way she laughed, her favorite food. After Chloe died, I remembered the way Chloe would spritz her perfume into the air three good times then walk into the mist. Simple, everyday things that made them the person they were in your eyes. Even now, I remember the expert way Rachel cooked in high heels.

Then, with all the memories comes the guilt. You remember

all the opportunities you had—and missed—to show them you loved them. Did they know? Did they *really* know how much I cared about them? I berated myself all the time when Dad died. I could have been so much nicer. I could have helped him more with little things. Like wash his car without complaining for once. When he left his coffee cup in the sink, would it have killed me to just wash it and put it away? I could have listened better when he talked about his childhood. Told him "I love you" without him having to tell me first.

This, the guilt, will be the hardest part for Galen. He already takes responsibility for so much that isn't his fault. He will somehow blame himself for Rachel's death. He will fall into a spiral of remorse, into a self-made pit of regret.

And I silently promise him to catch him when he does.

The Trackers around us work in respectful silence, gathering the human survivors together in boats, ready to send them on their way to the next island. The original plan was to swim them over, but since a few of the boats could be salvaged, it was decided that it would be best to let them go alone. After all, they have a fantastic story to tell, and chauffeuring them along would only lend credibility to it.

When boats take off, Grom motions for everyone to submerge. We follow quietly and gather around him at the bottom of the ocean. Only Galen remains at the surface. And Rachel.

"This area is off limits to our kind," Grom says. "Humans have seen us here, and their stories will spread to more humans. Some will believe them, some will not. Those that do might come to investigate. We will not give them anything to find here."

His command is met with solemn nods. "You must also

realize," he continues, "that it is only a matter of time now before this happens again. Maybe not in our generation, maybe not in the next. But the time is coming when humans will find us. We all must think about what this means for us individually, but most importantly, for our kind. Go home now to your families. Tell them what has happened. Talk with them about what might."

The crowd of Trackers and other volunteers disperses and we are left alone with one another and our thoughts.

Mom wraps her arms around me, careful to avoid my wound. "How are you holding up?" she whispers. I shrug. There is truth in a shrug. The truth is that there is no answer.

"Me, too," Mom says. "Me, too."

"I think Toraf should come to Galen's house to recover," Rayna says to Grom. There is no fight left in her. Just words and feelings. "I think we should ask Dr. Milligan to come look at him."

Grom nods. He is not in the mood for conflict, either. "I think you're right, little sister." He motions to the Trackers who hold an unconscious Toraf in their arms. "Take Princess Rayna and her mate wherever she bids you." He turns to his sister and presses a quick kiss to her forehead. "Send word if you need anything from me."

Mom had wrapped Toraf's side with seaweed to stave off the bleeding, but a small red stain is starting to soak through. He had a close call and we all know it. Just because his organs were spared doesn't mean his muscles will heal correctly. I hadn't thought of calling Dr. Milligan. I'm glad Rayna did. Besides,

Dr. Milligan will want to be updated on all the latest events. And we have to tell him about Rachel.

Rayna throws her arms around Grom in a fierce, short hug. "I will. I really will."

This chokes me up a bit. Even Mom appreciates the obvious upgrade in their relationship—and she doesn't even like Rayna. She gives my shoulder another squeeze. I pat her hand and lean into her. We've all been through so much. But we've been through it together. Even Grom and Rayna are grateful for each other today.

When Rayna and the Trackers leave, Grom glances topside. Then he lets his gaze settle on me. "Young Emma." It doesn't sound condescending at all, the way he says it. Just wistful. "The twins will need you now. More than they realize." He eases closer to me, pensive. "It was difficult for them when we lost our mother. Losing Rachel is . . . They suffered a great loss today."

I draw in a breath. If we weren't underwater, tears would be spilling down my cheeks instead of getting sopped up by the gentle current. I wonder how many tears the ocean has swallowed, how much of the ocean is actually made of tears.

"Grom, I hate to ask something like this, but what will we do with her body?" Mom says.

"What do humans normally do with their dead?"

"They bury them on land, or burn them. But the humans have rules and restrictions on that sort of thing. And Rachel wasn't exactly . . . Rachel has a complicated past. A past that makes it impossible to properly bury her."

I can tell this has already been weighing on Grom's mind. Is this the sort of thing adults think about when someone dies, to take care of these matters first and grieve later? A look of understanding passes between Grom and my mom. "I'll talk to the council about the Tomb Chamber," he says. "I hardly think they'll put up much of a resistance after today."

"I would like that," Galen says from behind his brother. I swim to him and he meets me halfway. His big arms encircle me. It's not a bear hug, or a sensual touch. It feels like Galen is clinging to me for dear life. Like he is caught in a riptide and I am his anchor.

"I'm so sorry," I whisper into his neck. The words almost lodge in my throat. He clutches me to him tighter, and rests his chin on the top of my hair.

"Woden has her," he tells Grom. "Until we decide what's best."

Grom doesn't answer. In fact, after a few minutes, I sense the pulses of Mom and Grom moving away from us. After several more minutes, I can't sense them at all. The only pulse I feel is Galen's. It drums against me, through me, around me.

Things will change without Rachel. Life will not run as smoothly. But this will not change. The way we fit together. The way we know each other.

Epilogue

"YOU'RE SURE you want to do this," Galen says, eyeing me like I've grown a tiara of snakes on my head.

"Absolutely." I unstrap the four-hundred-dollar silver heels and spike them into the sand. When he starts unraveling his tie, I throw out my hand. "No! Leave it. Leave everything on."

Galen frowns. "Rachel would kill us both. In our sleep. She would torture us first."

"This is our prom night. Rachel would want us to enjoy ourselves." I pull the thousand-or-so bobby pins from my hair and toss them in the sand. Really, both of us are right. She *would* want us to be happy. But she would also want us to stay in our designer clothes.

Leaning over, I shake my head like a wet dog, dispelling the magic of hairspray. Tossing my hair back, I look at Galen.

His crooked smile almost melts me where I stand. I'm just

glad to see a smile on his face at all. The last six months have been rough. "Your mother will want pictures," he tells me.

"And what will she do with pictures? There aren't exactly picture frames in the Royal Caverns." Mom's decision to mate with Grom and live as his queen didn't surprise me. After all, I am eighteen years old, an adult, and can take care of myself. Besides, she's just a swim away.

"She keeps picture frames at her house though. She could still enjoy them while she and Grom come to shore to—"

"Okay, ew. Don't say it. That's where I draw the line."

Galen laughs and takes off his shoes. I forget all about Mom and Grom. Galen, barefoot in the sand, wearing an Armani tux. What more could a girl ask for?

"Don't look at me like that, angelfish," he says, his voice husky. "Disappointing your grandfather is the last thing I want to do."

My stomach cartwheels. Swallowing doesn't help. "I can't admire you, even from afar?" I can't quite squeeze enough innocence in there to make it believable, to make it sound like I wasn't thinking the same thing he was.

Clearing his throat, he nods. "Let's get on with this." He closes the distance between us, making foot-size potholes with his stride. Grabbing my hand, he pulls me to the water. At the edge of the wet sand, just out of reach of the most ambitious wave, we stop.

"You're sure?" he says again.

"More than sure," I tell him, giddiness swimming through my veins like a sneaking eel. Images of the conference center downtown spring up in my mind. Red and white balloons, streamers, a loud, cheesy DJ yelling over the starting chorus of the next song. Kids grinding against one another on the dance floor to lure the chaperones' attention away from a punch bowl just waiting to be spiked. Dresses spilling over with skin, matching corsages, awkward gaits due to six-inch heels. The prom Chloe and I dreamed of.

But the memories I wanted to make at that prom died with Chloe. There could never be any joy in that prom without her. I couldn't walk through those doors and not feel that something was missing. A big something.

No, this is where I belong now. No balloons, no loud music, no loaded punch bowl. Just the quiet and the beach and Galen. This is my new prom. And for someone reason, I think Chloe would approve.

He nods once, firmly. "Okay."

Taking both of my hands, he pulls me into the tide. Salt water deepens the lavender satin of my gown to almost black. The waves push into it, making it heavier and heavier. "Tell me when," he says.

I nod. When Galen is neck deep and I'm clinging to him to keep my head above water. When my saturated prom dress feels like an anchor grasping at my limbs. When the moon is directly overhead and makes the silver flecks in his eyes shimmer like gems. That's when I'm ready. "Now," I breathe.

He brushes his lips against mine. Once. Twice. So soft it barely feels like anything. But it also feels like everything. He pulls me under. One day, when Galen and I are mated, I'll be a princess. But I'll never feel more like a princess than right now, in his arms, dancing on the ocean floor.

He pulls me from my trance with his lips against my ear. "Emma."

It's silly how my own name can send tingles shooting everywhere. "Hmm?"

"I've been thinking. About us." He pulls away from me. "I think . . . I think I need a distraction."

"Um. A distraction? From me?" The words taste vinegary in my mouth. They turn sweet again when Galen throws his head back and laughs.

"Emma," he says, brushing his thumb across my bottom lip. "You are the one thing I'm sure of. Completely. Without thinking twice. But I want to get away from here for a little while. And I want you to come with me. I know you're set on going to college in the fall. I'm only asking for the summer. Let's go somewhere. Do something."

I float up until I'm eye level with him. "Let's. Where will we go?"

He shrugs. "I don't care, as long as it's away from any ocean."

"So . . . the desert?"

He grimaces. "The mountains?"

I laugh. "Deal. We'll go to the mountains."

"You're sure?"

I pull him by the neck until our noses touch. "Completely. Without thinking twice."

Thank you for reading this **FEIWEL AND FRIENDS** book.
The Friends who made

OF TRITON

possible are:

Jean Feiwel	publisher
Liz Szabla	editor in chief
Rich Deas	creative director
Holly West	associate editor
Dave Barrett	executive managing editor
Nicole Liebowitz Moulaison	production manager
LAUREN A. BURNIAC	editor
Anna Roberto	assistant editor
Ashley Halsey	designer

FIND OUT MORE ABOUT OUR AUTHORS
AND ARTISTS AND OUR FUTURE
PUBLISHING AT
MACTEENBOOKS.COM.

OUR BOOKS ARE
FRIENDS FOR LIFE